Julie White

D0943136

sononis
PRESS
WINLAW, BRITISH COLUMBIA

Library and Archives Canada Cataloguing in Publication
White, Julie, 1958-
    Riding through fire / Julie White.
ISBN 978-1-55039-199-2
    I. Title.
PS8645.H54R53 2012   jC813'.6   C2012-901960-7

Sono Nis Press most gratefully acknowledges support for our publishing program
provided by the Government of Canada through the Canada Book Fund and
the Canada Council for the Arts, and by the Province of British Columbia
through the British Columbia Arts Council and the Book Publishing Tax Credit,
Ministry of Provincial Revenue.

Edited by Laura Peetoom
Copy edited by Dawn Loewen
Proofread by Audrey McClelland
Author photo by Andrea Blair, Paper Horse Photography

Published by
SONO NIS PRESS
Box 160
Winlaw, BC V0G 2J0
1-800-370-5228

Distributed in the U.S. by
Orca Book Publishers
Box 468
Custer, WA 98240-0468
1-800-210-5277

books@sononis.com
www.sononis.com

Printed and bound in Canada by Houghton Boston Printing.

Printed on acid-free paper that is forest friendly
(100% post-consumer recycled paper)
and has been processed chlorine free.

The Canada Council | Le Conseil des Arts
for the Arts | du Canada

*To all who have ever dedicated time,
energy and resources to the rescue
and care of horses in need*

1

Something was under the bed.

Kirsty jerked awake. As her thudding heart slowed, she could hear muffled scrabbling and rapid panting. She pushed herself up on her elbows. Her curtains billowed in the warm wind gusting through the screen of her open window.

A flare of light illuminated her bedroom. Moments later thunder rumbled. The panting grew louder. She leaned over the side of her bed. Deep in the dark recesses she caught the gleam of a pair of eyes.

"Jet," she sighed.

Another flash of lightning. Barely a second later, thunder boomed, rattling the window glass. Jet clawed at the old wood floorboards. He squirmed out from under the bed and scrambled in beside her.

"Hey, old man, take it easy." Kirsty wrapped her arm around the elderly Labrador and felt him trembling underneath her. "Don't be scared. I'm here. It's just a summer storm."

A tall figure in a flowing white gown drifted through her open door. It floated across her room and leaned over her bed.

"Hi, Mom."

The figure sprang back. "Kirsty! You startled me! I thought you were asleep."

"Jet woke me."

"Poor old dog. He must be terrified." Mom sat down on Kirsty's bed. "Listen. Do you hear it?"

A faint pinging on the metal roof. "Rain!"

"At last." Mom glided to the window, slid off the screen and stuck her head outside. "Oh, thank goodness."

Kirsty slipped from her bed and joined her. Carried by the wind, a smattering of raindrops softly pelted their faces. Kirsty held out her hands, palms up, expecting the light sting of rain. She felt nothing. She rubbed her hands together. They were dry.

Beside her, she heard Mom's disappointed sigh.

Another riffle of wind eddied around them, blowing Kirsty's hair across her face. The crash of thunder was distant and hollow. The storm had blown on.

And with it any chance of rain.

Just after seven on a Monday morning, and the air was already growing warm. Kirsty sat cross-legged in the long, dusty grass at the end of the driveway, keeping watch. She heard the rumble of an engine climbing the hill. Moments later, Lucy March's pickup came into view towing the horse trailer.

Kirsty waited to approach until the clouds of road dust skirting the truck and trailer settled down. Lucy rolled down her window. "Morning, Kirsty. Ready to go?"

"I sure am! I'll just check on the ponies." Kirsty stepped up on the running board of the horse trailer and regarded the two long faces inside the grilles. She slipped her hand through and stroked the ragged white blaze of the pinto. "Hey, Lancelot. How're you doing, boy? Up for an adventure?"

The pony twitched an ear and resumed munching hay from a canvas feed bag. Kirsty hopped down and went around to the truck's passenger door. Lucy waited until she'd fastened her seat belt before putting the truck into gear.

"Wait! Hold on!" Mom ran down the driveway in her housecoat and gumboots. Lucy set her foot down on the brake. "I just heard on the radio that the lightning started two fires near Falkland last night."

Lucy nodded. "They're up in the mountains on the other side of the valley—a long way from where we're going to be. Right now, the wind is blowing the fire back into the mountains." She reached through the open window and patted Mom's shoulder. "Don't worry, Linda. I wouldn't take your girl into danger."

Mom's eyes searched Lucy's face. She let out a sigh. "Of course you wouldn't, Lucy. It's the weather—all this heat. It makes me edgy."

"I know what you mean. It's more like midsummer than the end of September. Let's pray that we get rain… and soon."

"Amen to that! All right, you two, have a good day. Get those cows rounded up! Be careful, okay?"

"We will, Mom. See you tonight!" Kirsty waved as they drove away. Settling back in her seat, she noticed her left wrist was bare, revealing a pale bracelet of untanned skin. She'd forgotten her watch.

"Now, tell me again why you don't have school today," said Lucy.

"It's an in-service day for the teachers. They have school and we get the day off."

"But you just started classes a few weeks ago." Lucy clucked her tongue. "In my day we went to class every day of the school year—students and teachers."

"Things are different now," said Kirsty.

"They sure are." Lucy fell silent, thinking of times past.

The Hallidays' ranch was a slow, winding, half-hour drive away. Kirsty bounced in her seat, impatient at Lucy's cautious driving.

"Hang on to some of that energy; you might need it

later," Lucy advised, steering around the steep corner of a switchback. "It's going to be a long day. And a real warm one."

Kirsty forced herself still. She stared out at the stands of evergreens, their needles dull from weeks of drought. Her face was already prickling with sweat from the rising sun beating in through the windshield of the truck.

"You're quiet," observed Lucy.

"Lucy, I've never been on a cattle drive before."

"I know. You'll do fine, Kirsty."

"But I've only had Lancelot for just over six months."

"I know that, too. Listen, girl, no one's going to ask you to do anything you're not capable of doing. You'll just tag along at the back of the herd with me, keeping them bunched together and moving."

"That doesn't sound too hard."

"It's not. The older cows know what's up because it happens every year. The only difference is we're bringing them down a month early because the grass is all grazed down on the range." The narrow road flattened out. Lucy pulled up to a stop sign and glanced over at Kirsty. "You've had a lot of new experiences the last few months. This is just another one of them."

"A new experience," Kirsty repeated.

"That's right. A chance to find out what you're made of." Lucy crossed the intersection and geared down to climb the hill on the other side. "And to discover who you're becoming."

It wasn't long before they'd pulled into a bumpy driveway leading into a ranch yard packed with corrals and weathered buildings.

"Lucy, thank you so much for coming out to give us a hand." A man with a cowboy hat pulled low on his head came up to the horse trailer as Kirsty unloaded Lancelot. He was leading a stout chestnut horse, and spurs jingled on the heels of his boots.

"My pleasure, Stuart." Lucy tied her mare Blackbird to the side of the trailer. "I'm looking forward to it, to tell you the truth. It'll be good to be riding out in those hills. This is my young friend Kirsty Hagen."

Stuart Halliday lifted his hat. "Pleased to meet you, Kirsty. This is my wife, Midge. A lot of folks would call her my better half. They'd be right, too."

A lady with crow-black hair peeking out from under her straw hat rode up on a buckskin. "Lucy March, how good it is to see you! Now you realize, don't you, this whole drive was planned as an excuse to get you over here."

"I suspected as much, Midge," laughed Lucy. "We have got to get together more often."

"And how is that granddaughter of yours? What's this I hear about her riding in the Olympics?"

"Not the Olympics, not just yet. She's in Alberta, riding in a big horse show at Spruce Meadows. Doing good, too. She won a class day before yesterday."

"Oh my goodness, you must be so proud."

"I am indeed. I just wish we'd see more of her. Since she started riding for Laurence Devries, she's been competing just about every weekend and sometimes during the week."

"That's a hectic schedule for a young girl."

Lucy nodded. "It sure is. But it's a great opportunity for Faye."

"What about school?"

"She's doing that online. At least I hope she's keeping up with her courses. Schoolwork's never been Faye's strong point."

"I'll bet you miss her. How are you managing on the farm without her help?"

"Well, Riley's taking a year off before starting college, but he's working full-time. Kirsty here helps me a lot. Don't know what I'd do without her."

Midge turned her bright smile on Kirsty. A fine network of lines bracketed the corners of her mouth. Despite her slim build and erect posture, she wasn't a young woman. Not quite Lucy's age, perhaps, but certainly years older than Kirsty's mother. "Hi there, Kirsty. So you're stepping into Faye's shoes, are you?"

Kirsty ducked her head, certain these people were

humouring her. "I'm doing my best."

Midge nodded in approval. "That's all anyone can ask."

"I haven't had my pony very long. I don't know if he's herded cattle before. *I* sure haven't." That was the thing about following in Faye's footsteps—everyone expected her to be just as experienced. Kirsty hadn't been brought up on horseback, not like Faye. She'd learned a lot in the few months since Lancelot and the Marches had come into her life, but it was just enough to show her how much more she needed to know.

"Kirsty, I can tell you've got a good head on your shoulders—that's all that'll be needed today. And your pony's a solid sort with a real nice eye; he'll do just fine in the mountains." Midge smiled at her encouragingly.

"Now, you're not planning to ride all day in that little pancake of a saddle, are you?" asked Stuart Halliday. He frowned at the English saddle Kirsty had placed on Lancelot's back.

"It's all I have."

"You'd be a lot more comfortable in a stock saddle. We can lend you one. Jesse! We need a saddle over here. Auntie Mandy's old one, that you used to ride in. Make sure it's got a pair of saddlebags tied on."

"What do you think, Lucy?" asked Kirsty. "Should I change saddles?"

"I think so. A stock saddle is designed for riding all day

doing this kind of work."

Kirsty lifted her saddle off and carefully stowed it on the rack inside the trailer. A scowling, skinny-limbed boy of about fifteen packed a wide-skirted saddle over. Lancelot started as the boy flung the big saddle on his back.

"Easy, boy, easy," cautioned Stuart. "Set it on the horse's back, Jesse, don't throw it."

Jesse squinted his eyes at the old man and turned to leave.

"Hang on there a moment. You remember our grandson Jesse, don't you, Lucy? Marla's boy?" said Midge.

"Of course I do! I haven't seen you since you were eight or nine, son. How old are you now, Jesse?"

"Fifteen," he muttered. He flipped his dark hair back with a jerk of his head. "Nearly."

"Jesse's spending some time here on the ranch. His birthday's in October," said Stuart. "We're throwing a big party for him. You and Kirsty will have to come."

Jesse rolled his eyes behind his grandfather's back.

"That sounds like a whole lot of fun, doesn't it, Kirsty?" said Lucy.

"It does. Excuse me, but I don't know how to do up this girth." She pointed to the wide band of wool strings woven together.

"Cinch," Jesse said. "It's called a cinch." He reached under Lancelot's belly and caught the metal ring on the end of the cinch. Tugging free a long leather strap attached to the saddle, he deftly looped the strap through the ring several times and finished up with a flat knot. "Check it after you've been riding awhile. You might have to tighten it."

"How do I do that?" asked Kirsty.

He sighed. "Do what I just did. You were watching, weren't you?"

"I couldn't see very well. You went too fast."

Jesse's eyes rolled again, like dark marbles. "Get someone to help you." He turned his back and walked away.

"Thank you!" Kirsty called after him. No one could accuse *her* of bad manners. "What a pain," she added under her breath.

She noticed the stock saddle had two big canvas pockets tied behind the seat with thick leather strings so they rested on top of the saddle skirts. She undid the rusting buckles of the nearest one and peeked inside to find it empty.

"What are these?" she asked.

"They're saddlebags, for carrying supplies," Lucy explained. "It's going to be a long ride. We'll each need some provisions and something to pack them in."

Lucy had Blackbird saddled and bridled and was preparing to mount up. Kirsty copied her motions, twisting the stiff, wide-skirted stirrup and sliding her boot in. She hopped aboard, settling gently into the broad, built-up seat that felt more like a chair than a saddle.

"Feel strange?" Lucy grinned over at her.

"Does it ever!" Kirsty squirmed, trying to find her balance. "It's so big. I don't know where to sit."

"You'll get used to it. Come on, we've got a few minutes before we move out. I'll show you around."

They rode past a modest, squarely built white house with a red tin roof. Wild rose bushes pressed protectively against its walls, and a huge weeping willow, brittle branched and yellowing, still provided a measure of shade on the western side. The ponies' hooves rang out on hardpan, baked to cement. Lucy pulled up beside a network of stout log corrals and gestured to the view beyond. "You can see why they call this Mountainridge Ranch."

"It's beautiful," said Kirsty.

They were on a flat-topped ridge, partway up a mountainside. Ahead of them rolled away acres and acres of dusty grey fields randomly patched with groves of firs and brown-tipped cedar. Below the flats, a narrow silver river glinted between stands of shrivelled willow on the valley floor. Straight across from them the far side of the valley, densely forested with dark evergreens, rose steeply to the cloudless blue sky. Except for a few horses in one of the pastures, there wasn't an animal in sight.

Kirsty sighed. If only she had grandparents or other close family with a ranch she could visit, riding the range and herding cattle. All her relatives—the few she had—

were city people with boring office jobs. She looked around.

"Where are the cows?" she asked.

Lucy twisted around, nodding her chin at the heavily treed mountain rising behind them. "Up there."

"How are we going to find them in all those trees?"

"We do a lot of looking. Stuart and Midge know where to start searching, but I expect we've got a big job ahead of us. Most likely the cows have spread out, trying to find grass."

A whistle split the air.

"Come on, that's for us." Lucy led the way past a hay barn packed to the rafters with enormous round bales just about as tall as Kirsty. They came up on the far side of the house where a group of ten riders had gathered on the ranch driveway, including Jesse on a stout black horse. Midge was passing out water and lunch food. Kirsty took two bottles of water and a sandwich.

"Better have two," said Midge, slipping a second sandwich into a saddlebag. She fastened the buckle for Kirsty. "Whew, these old buckles are rusty. Time to replace them."

"Okay, let's head out!" called Stuart.

Lucy and Kirsty moved their mounts to the back of the group. A pair of lean-framed border collies darted back and forth beside the horses, yipping in excitement.

"Spark, Fly, quiet! Come with me, Kirsty, so you can meet these folks." Stuart moved his horse through the line with Kirsty beside him, introducing her to the other riders, many of whom were neighbours. They reached the last rider. "And you already know Jesse. Now, that's a lot of names to put to faces, but by the end of the day you'll have everyone sorted out."

An ageless cowboy on a bay Appaloosa doffed his hat. "Nice-looking mount you've got there."

Kirsty beamed. "Thank you…"—she searched for his name—"Larry." Another rancher on the flats, who shared the range with the Hallidays.

"He looks like he'll go all day without turning a hair."

"I…I don't know. I hope he can. I've never done anything like this before."

Larry's weathered gaze regarded her steadily. "You'll do fine, Kirsty." He backed up his words with a slow nod of his head.

"You'll probably enjoy the company of someone closer to your own age than old fossils like us," said Stuart, "so we'll leave you here with Jesse. I'll go on up ahead to open the gate."

Jesse cut his horse in front of Lancelot. "I'll do it, Grandpa."

"Well, thank you, son. Much appreciated."

The riders crossed the main road and passed through the open wire gate on the far side, pulling up to wait for Jesse to wrestle the gate shut.

"Jesse, before you mount up, check Kirsty's cinch, will you?" requested Midge. "Make sure it's good and snug before we start climbing."

"Sorry, I forgot," Kirsty apologized as Jesse tugged the slack out of the cinch.

Without replying, he swung aboard his horse.

"Let's go!" The leaders urged their horses up the steeply inclined track, wide enough for only two riders side by side. The air here was still fresh and cool, lightly scented with resin from the firs lining the trail. Lancelot grunted as Jesse's horse bumped him, squeezing past.

"Whatever happened to 'excuse me'?" Kirsty muttered softly. She reached around the saddle horn to stroke her pony's neck.

"Jesse!" His grandfather hailed him when he was nearly at the front of the ride. "Stick with Kirsty, make sure she's okay."

Glowering, Jesse pulled up his horse at the side of the trail and let the other riders pass before falling in beside Lancelot and Kirsty.

"You don't have to," she told him. "I'm fine."

He snorted contemptuously, his eyes revolving in their sockets again. "Yeah, right." He stilled his eyes long enough to cast a pointed look at her pony's cinch.

Kirsty flushed. She scrolled through a list of retorts in her mind, trying to choose the best one.

"How's it going back there, Kirsty?" Lucy called from the middle of the pack. "You doing okay?"

These are Lucy's friends, Kirsty reminded herself. *I am an invited guest.* She took a deep breath. "I'm good!" she shouted back with forced cheerfulness. She gave Jesse a bared-teeth smile. "Really good."

Jesse's eyes rolled again.

You keep doing that, Kirsty thought, *and one day your eyeballs are going to spin right out of your head.*

For Lucy's sake she would try her hardest to get along with this surly boy. "So what's your horse's name?" she asked.

"Quincy."

"This is Lancelot."

When Jesse said nothing, she waded on. "Have you had Quincy a long time?"

"He's not mine."

"Oh, who does he belong to?"

"My grandparents."

"Have *they* had him a long time?"

"All his life."

"Wow! Was he born on the ranch? Did they have his dam?" Kirsty remembered the correct term for a mother horse.

"Yes and yes." Jesse held up his hand like a stop sign. "Look, quit with all the questions, will you? We've got a long climb ahead of us; save your breath for that."

Well, I tried to be friendly, Kirsty told herself.

The incline seemed nearly vertical now, the horses low-headed as they climbed it. Kirsty leaned forward, giving Lancelot a long rein and standing in her stirrups to take her weight out of the saddle. She wanted to pull up to give him a breather, but when she tightened the reins he shook his head in protest. He was determined to keep up with the herd.

Kirsty pulled her feet free of the stirrups and, grabbing the horn, vaulted from the saddle. Reaching up, she held the reins in one hand and the horn in the other. Pulled along by her pony, she hiked up the trail. In just a few steps she was huffing and puffing as hard as he was.

"What are you doing?" demanded Jesse. "Did you fall off?"

"No! I'm helping my pony get up the hill."

Jesse slapped his hand to his forehead. "Listen, Kirsty, it seems you're kind of mixed up. We walk *dogs*; we *ride* horses."

"Ha ha, very funny," she gasped.

After a while he turned his horse, blocking Lancelot's path. "Get back on, okay? That pony's a lot fitter than you are."

Kirsty's legs were trembling, her breath roaring into her lungs through her open mouth. Jesse was right; she was blowing a lot harder than Lancelot. Fumbling her boot into the stirrup, she dragged herself up the side of the saddle, struggling to lift her right leg over the high-backed cantle. Lancelot wiggled impatiently, but Jesse kept him in place. Finally she got her leg over and settled into the saddle. Jesse moved aside.

"You are the craziest girl," he said.

Before Kirsty could reply, Lancelot bounded up the hill, eager to catch up with the others. Jesse whooped his horse up beside him. Barely a minute later the trail levelled off and the ride pulled up to rest their mounts.

"Are you kids doing okay back there?" asked Midge. "I hope you're not eating too much dust."

Jesse shrugged and said nothing.

"We're fine, Mrs. Halliday," said Kirsty.

"Call me Midge." She undid the bandana around her neck and passed it to Kirsty. "Tie this around the lower half of your face. That's right, so it covers your nose and mouth. There, now you've got a mask to keep out the dust."

The pointed end of the folded bandana was hanging down past Kirsty's chin. "Now I feel like an outlaw in a western."

"Jesse, Kirsty here's from the big city too. Vancouver, Lucy tells me."

"Delta, actually, but it's close to Vancouver," said Kirsty, her voice muffled by the bandana. "My mom and I moved to Armstrong last year."

"How are you liking country life so far?"

"Oh, I love it. I never want to live in the city again."

"I'm with you there, Kirsty. It sounds like you're a girl after my own heart."

"Why don't you adopt *her*, Grandma," snarled Jesse suddenly. "Then everyone can be where they want." He spun his horse around and headed off into the forest.

"Jesse! Where do you think you're going?" Stuart bellowed after him.

"Call of nature!"

Midge's mouth tightened into a thin line. Her eyes met Lucy's and she shook her head. "That boy! I just keep telling myself, give him time. He'll come around."

"He will. Underneath all the attitude, he's a good kid."

"He is," Midge agreed, "but he made some bad choices."

Kirsty waited for Midge to say more.

Midge lifted her eyes. "Well, right now I'm counting my blessings: a good horse under me, friends around me and the blue sky overhead. I am a fortunate woman. Come on, folks, let's ride."

2

It took the best part of two hours before they came out at the top of the mountain, the trees parting to encompass a natural meadow. A few white-faced cows, most of them with red bodies, were bedded down in the shade, their half-grown calves nearby in a nursery group. They lumbered to their feet, bawling, as the riders approached.

"Not a blade of grass left," said Lucy, looking down at the yellow stubble.

"It's bad." Stuart Halliday shook his head. "As bad as I've ever seen in over thirty years of running on this range. Whoa, now, steady."

The horses startled in their tracks as a small herd of deer burst from the trees and pogo-sticked across the meadow, their bushy white tails flipped up over their backs.

Lancelot scooted a couple of feet sideways along with the other horses, setting Kirsty's heart thumping in her chest. She snatched at the reins but the pony had settled, his head high to watch as the deer vanished into the forest.

She let out a long sigh of relief. Looking down, she

realized she had one hand wrapped around the saddle horn. She made herself unlock her fingers and let go.

"We call that 'grabbing leather,'" said Jesse. He was slouched in his saddle, smirking. "Hey, don't be embarrassed; better to do that than fall off."

He grinned at Kirsty's glare, then swung his horse around to follow the other riders as they skirted the meadow to pick up the track on the far side.

Kirsty blinked furiously, her eyes prickling. She would not let Jesse Halliday make her cry. At the moment there was nothing she longed for more than Faye's company and steadfast support. Her friend had been there when Kirsty had fallen from Lancelot just months before and badly sprained her wrist after the pony had been spooked by a deer. She would have understood the fear that had Kirsty clutching the saddle horn. Faye's sympathy would be brisk, just like her grandmother's, but it would be sincere.

She sure wouldn't have found it funny, like Jesse just had.

He was probably the most horrible person she'd ever met, Kirsty decided, holding Lancelot back to let Jesse get well ahead. It was hard to believe such nice people as Midge and Stuart Halliday could have a grandson like him.

Sometimes, for some people, life just wasn't very fair.

The track had levelled out. Through a gap in the trees, she saw the middle group of riders angling back toward her as the track curved sharply. Kirsty seized the chance to escape Jesse's irritating presence. She directed Lancelot to take a shortcut through the forest, urging him through the crackling brush to join up with the other riders. Now she was well ahead of Jesse.

"Kirsty! Everything okay?" Lucy asked as she emerged from the trees.

"Yes, I just wanted to ride with you." She squeezed her pony between Lucy's and Midge's mounts, then yanked the bandana down around her neck.

"Where's Jesse?"

"Oh, he's back there somewhere."

"I hope he's remembered his manners," said Midge.

Kirsty hesitated for just a second before nodding. "He's explained a few things to me."

"Oh, good, I'm glad he's being helpful."

She looked relieved, and Kirsty was glad she'd dressed up the truth instead of telling her that Jesse was actually being a complete jerk.

"All those cows back in that meadow—why did we leave them behind?"

"We'll pick them up on the way back," Midge told her. "Pretty soon we're going to spread out and start gathering. You watch, some of the old ladies will know what's going on and start heading down on their own. Of course, there's always one or two that just can't go along with the rest of the herd. Keep your eyes open for a speckle-faced cow; she's the worst one for wandering off. She'll have a calf with her."

"Always has to be a troublemaker in every crowd," observed Lucy.

I'll second that, Kirsty thought a short while later when once again Jesse was assigned as her partner. She regretted giving Midge the false impression that they were getting along. The riders were splitting up to search the bush for cattle and push them to the road.

"Take the old logging road and go as far as the cut-block—you know the one I'm talking about, Jesse?" said Stuart.

"Yeah, yeah, I remember."

"You okay, just the two of you? Want another rider along?"

"I can manage, Grandpa. Give me some credit. I've done this how many times before?"

"Jesse." Stuart injected a warning into his grandson's name.

"In fact, I'll be a lot better off without some greenhorn along," Jesse went on. "Put her with someone else."

"That's fine with me," said Kirsty quickly. "I don't mind."

"Jesse," Stuart Halliday repeated. His eyes met the boy's and held.

Jesse looked away first. "Whatever! Have it your way.

But she's got to keep up. I'm not doing any babysitting."

"Maybe I *should* go with someone else," said Kirsty. "I really don't know what to do." She sent Lucy a pleading look.

"You'll pick it up quick," said Lucy.

"But you said—"

Lucy edged Blackbird alongside Lancelot and set a hand on Kirsty's shoulder. "You're ready for this, girl. You can do it."

"You think so?"

"I know so." She winked and moved off.

Kirsty squared her shoulders and looked around. All the riders were breaking up into pairs and moving out.

Jesse started off into the forest without waiting to see if Kirsty was following. She hustled Lancelot after him. As she got close she heard him muttering, "One little screw-up, just one, and everyone's treating you like an idiot."

"Were you talking to me?"

"No."

"What *is* your problem?" she said under her breath.

"Huh?"

"Oh, nothing," Kirsty said airily. "I didn't say a thing."

Jesse narrowed his eyes before looking away.

Branches slapped Kirsty's face as they wove through the trees. They scrambled up a steep slope and came out on an overgrown logging road.

"Hold up. My pony needs to catch his breath."

"I'm going ahead. You come along when you're good and ready."

"Hey, don't leave me!"

He twisted around in the saddle to look back at her. "All you have to do is follow the road. Don't worry, all the noise you've been making has probably scared off most of the bears."

And with that, he waved cheerily and disappeared around a bend in the road.

3

"Jesse Halliday, you are the most annoying person I've ever met," Kirsty muttered to the empty road.

She was tempted to turn Lancelot around and head back to tell Midge and Stuart just how their grandson was behaving. She sat on her blowing pony imagining how that scene would play out and couldn't come up with a version that didn't have her sounding like a whining little kid. Besides, the other riders were spread out through the bush, and she couldn't be sure of finding them.

The trees hemming them in all around made it impossible to make out any landmarks to place herself. She recalled the journey to this point and realized that, except for the big meadow, all she could remember were trees and more trees. Right now, if she had to find her way off the mountain, she wouldn't know what direction to go except back down the road.

A small breeze sighed through the dry needles of the fir tree beside her, the only sound or movement around her since Jesse had left them. Except for her pony, she was completely alone.

Lancelot stomped a foot, impatient to move on. His breathing had slowed to nearly normal, so Kirsty clucked to him. He shot off up the road.

His ears, Kirsty noticed, were swivelling back and forth.

Something brushed the back of her bare neck. She swatted at it with her hand and came up with nothing. Her neck tickled again.

It could be only the wind, she told herself, swiping her fingers at an itchy spot just below her ear.

Pulling her hand away, she discovered a tiny lump of grey dirt under her fingernail. It was surprisingly warm from the heat of the day. She touched the lump with her thumb and it crumbled to dust.

Kirsty brushed her fingers clean on her jeans and hitched the bandana up higher around her neck.

They rounded the bend and climbed another rise to a switchback. Still the road was empty. Kirsty tried to gain confidence from Lancelot's steady march—although his ears were still twisting about, he wasn't snorting or slowing up to sniff the air.

How far ahead could Jesse be? She tried to remember just how long they'd rested, but her sense of time was skewed by the stillness of the forest. She tipped her head back to view the empty blue sky stretched above the treetops. If the sun were directly overhead it would be noon, she knew that much, but the sun wasn't even in sight.

Lancelot braked abruptly, lifting his head high. He swung around to look down the road and snorted, the sound blasting through the quiet air like a rifle shot.

A loud snap reverberated through the forest. Suddenly the woods echoed with the crackling and rustling of trampled brush. Some large creature was forcing a path through the brittle undergrowth. She could hear the pant of its heavy breathing and then a long, low growl.

Lancelot trembled beneath her. Before she could hold him back, he bolted off down the road. She tugged at the reins but his neck was braced, his jaw locked against the bit. He skittered around the switchback with her clinging to the saddle horn with both hands.

Quincy clambered onto the road from the woods, directly in their path. Lancelot flung up his head. He braked sharply, pitching Kirsty onto his neck. He ducked to one side and she felt herself sliding, the weight of her upper body overpowering her grip on the horn.

Abruptly Lancelot jerked still. There was pressure against her knee and a hand blocking her shoulder. The hand pushed hard and she was back in the saddle.

Kirsty busied herself finding her stirrups again and taking up her reins. Her hands, she noticed, were shaking. She took a couple of deep breaths to slow down the pounding of her heart.

"You okay?" asked Jesse.

She nodded. "Thanks." She swallowed to wet her dry mouth. "I'm fine."

"Think you can manage him if I take my horse away?" He had Quincy tight against Lancelot. At Kirsty's nod he sidestepped the black quarter horse over, keeping a close eye on the pony.

"He's fine. It wasn't his fault. Something in the bush spooked him."

Jesse's eyes darted to hers, then away again.

"There's something in there, Jesse," she went on. "I heard it growl. Shouldn't we get away from here?" She heard her voice rising higher and higher. Her heart was thumping hard again.

"Listen, Kirsty, don't make a big fuss—"

"I heard it!" she insisted. "Come on, we've got to get out of here." She dug her heels into Lancelot, urging him down the trail.

"Hey, hold up there." Jesse caught the pony's bridle and turned him around. "We've got a job to do, remember?"

"We can't go back that way!"

"It's okay! There's no wild animal."

"Yes, there is!"

He shook his head. "No, that was me you heard coming through the bush."

"But...what were you doing down there? You were up

ahead."

"There's a fork a ways up. You weren't coming, so I decided to quickly check one road out and then double back through the woods to make sure you were okay."

"I heard something growl. It wasn't my imagination; I really did hear it."

He sighed. "Me again."

"What? All that growling was you? Why would you do something like that?"

"Just goofing around." He shrugged. "You know, trying to have some fun."

"That's what you call fun? Spooking my pony and scaring me half to death? You're crazy, you know that?"

"Oh, quit making such a big deal out of nothing."

"What if I'd gotten hurt? Would that be funny, too?"

"Well, you didn't, did you? And a greenhorn like you shouldn't be on such a spooky pony."

He started up the road again, checking back over his shoulder to make sure Kirsty was coming along.

Lancelot was rooting at the reins, eager to catch up with Quincy. Unless she wanted to argue with her pony the whole ride, she had to let him walk along with the bigger horse and his rider. Reluctantly she let him go.

For a half-hour or so they rode in silence, except for some tuneless whistling on Jesse's part. Kirsty fumed, Jesse's words churning around inside her. Finally, she couldn't hold back any longer.

"Look, I know he's not the best-trained pony in the world," she burst out, "but he's a lot better than he was when I got him. I'm not like you or Faye; I don't have grandparents with fields full of horses and ponies that I can pick and choose from. I bought Lancelot all by myself with my own money. And you can look down your nose at me all you want, Jesse Halliday, but don't you dare say anything bad about my pony, not ever again. Get it?"

Jesse looked over at her and slowly nodded. "Okay." He narrowed his eyes at Lancelot.

"What?"

"You really bought that pony all by yourself? Come on, your parents must have kicked in something."

"They didn't. It was just me. I look after him by myself, too. I work for Lucy to pay for his board."

"So your folks don't have money either."

"My parents are divorced." Even after all this time it was still hard to say. "My dad has a new family, and my mom, well, she doesn't make much money."

"That must suck."

Kirsty shrugged. She'd gotten used to the big changes in her life, including the sad parts. It helped to tell herself that all the upheaval and tearing apart had led her to Lancelot. The best thing had come along with the worst, part of a parcel.

"Well, it sounds like Lucy March has got herself a pretty sweet deal," Jesse said.

"What do you mean?"

"She gets free labour on the farm while her spoiled granddaughter is off playing. You must feel like Cinderella, slaving away while Faye March is having a fun time at the ball."

"No, I don't. I like working for Lucy. She teaches me a lot. And Faye is my friend."

Jesse snorted. "Some friend."

"Faye's a good friend."

"She is, huh? Then why aren't you at this horse show with her?"

"I'm not a good enough rider...yet. It's a really important horse show. Riders come from all over the world to compete in it."

"Just to ride in a horse show? That's nuts. Bet you it's not cheap. How can Faye March afford to go in something like that?"

"She's riding someone else's horses. He pays for everything, I think."

"Some people get all the luck." The familiar scowl settled over Jesse's face. "And the name's Sims, not Halliday."

"Are you sure it's not Grumpy?" Kirsty said, just loud enough for him to hear.

Jesse lapsed into his sullen silence again. This time Kirsty let him be.

After climbing a series of switchbacks, they came out into a logged-off area—Jesse called it a cutblock—where they found their first cattle grazing in a stand of replanted young trees at the far side.

"Stay here. I'll get in behind and push them onto the road. You make sure they keep together and head in the right direction," said Jesse.

"How do I do that?"

Jesse reined in his horse. "On second thought, just stay right there and don't do anything. Unless you get an angry mama cow coming at you. Then you might want to get out of the way."

"Ha ha, very funny."

"I mean it, Kirsty." He shot her a look over his shoulder as Quincy picked his way through the logging debris, leaving Kirsty wondering how seriously to take him. She waited at the edge of the cutblock.

The cattle seemed peaceable enough as, of their own accord, they meandered across the cutblock and lumbered down onto the dirt road, their sturdy calves trailing in their wake. The cows were bigger than she expected, nearly as tall as Lancelot. Some of the offspring were about the size of a Shetland pony. Kirsty kept her post on the side of the cutblock, but not one of the big red bodies made a move to head back into the bush. The broad white faces didn't even turn her way, much to her relief.

"Okay, that's all of them," said Jesse, joining up with her. His frown was gone, along with his earlier black mood.

"So now what?" she asked.

"Now we take them down the road—slowly."

"That's all?"

"Let's hope so." He smiled at the look on her face. "You were expecting this to be like something out of the movies, weren't you? A lot of yelling and chasing and running cattle."

"Well, yes, I was."

"Sorry, but it's not going to be that way at all. You're probably going to be bored to death. We want to keep these cows quiet and moving slow. There's no sense in feeding them all summer on mountain grass just to run off all their weight on the drive home."

"That's fine with me. How come you know so much about herding cows if you're a city kid?"

"My mom was raised on the ranch. I've been coming here for the summers since I was a baby. Except this last summer, I was supposed to be somewhere else."

"So why weren't you? And why are you here now?"

Jesse's forehead wrinkled again. "I don't want to talk about it."

"Whatever." Kirsty shrugged, pretending she wasn't at all curious.

She pulled the bandana up over her mouth to screen out the dust churned up by the cows and calves. Quincy and Lancelot settled into matched strides, swinging along in unison behind the long parade of blocky red cattle. The day was warming up quickly, the scent of resin from the conifer trees rising with the heat.

"It's going to be another hot one," Jesse said, swiping his brow as they rode through a patch of direct sunlight before the shade of the evergreens sheltered them again.

On command, a warm breeze wafted across their faces as they went into the second switchback. Kirsty sat up tall, sniffing the air.

"Do you smell smoke?"

Jesse checked. "Nothing but dust and cow patties."

"I can." She took in a deep breath through her nostrils. "It's stronger now."

"Must be from that fire over Falkland way. Hey, Freckle Face, you get back here! Stop her, Kirsty, don't let her get past you!"

A rangy cow with splatters of red across her white face ran straight at Lancelot. Kirsty dug in her heels, but the pony scrambled back out of the big cow's path. Freckle Face and her calf lumbered right past Lancelot's nose back into the forest. Inspired by the speckled cow's example, three or four other cows scattered into the trees after her.

"Why didn't you stop them?" demanded Jesse.

"I tried!"

"You just stood there! Hold the rest of the herd right here. Whatever you do, don't let them turn back."

"Jesse, no," she protested. "Please, I can't—"

But Jesse was already plunging into the timber, Quincy dodging in and out of trees after Freckle Face and her followers.

Kirsty slumped on her pony and struggled to hold in tears. She *had* tried, and she'd messed up. Lancelot had balked when she needed him. They were both failures, and she knew Jesse would make sure to tell everyone on the drive when they joined back up with it.

Beneath her, Lancelot shifted restlessly. Kirsty blinked away her tears and looked up to see that the cows at the rear had turned, and now curly white heads were facing her instead of long ropy tails. The rest of the herd was bunching up, turning back to press against the cows behind them.

Instantly she imagined Jesse's scorn if she let them get past her again.

"Get around," she squawked. "Come on, you cows, get going."

The cattle rolled their eyes, unimpressed. Their stout bodies pushed toward her and Lancelot.

In desperation, she waved her arms and hollered, urging Lancelot at the herd. He swerved, reluctant to confront the cows. Kirsty reached out and swatted one across the back with her bare hand. The cow shuffled sideways. She angled

Lancelot to go in again, but the cow retreated, keeping just out of reach.

Suddenly Lancelot's instincts switched on. He lunged at the cows and they scooted back. Kirsty felt his confidence pick up. Flat eared, the pony snaked his head, even nipping a rough-haired rump. The cow ducked away, shoving back the ones behind it. Lancelot dove at it again.

The tide began to turn. One by one, and then all together, cows twisted around. Encouraged, Kirsty whooped and yelled. The entire herd streamed down the road, the leaders breaking into a run.

In moments the herd was clumsily galloping down the road.

"Whoa," Kirsty shouted futilely. She slowed Lancelot. "Jesse!"

"Coming!" Hoofbeats drummed behind her. She looked over her shoulder and saw Jesse coming up behind her with the quitters. He pushed them past her into the back of the herd.

"They started running," Kirsty called. "I don't know how to stop them."

She felt her neck muscles tense as she waited for the telling-off Jesse was sure to give her.

"Back off, that's all we can do."

They pulled up their mounts, putting some distance between themselves and the herd before quietly walking after it.

"They all started turning around," Kirsty explained anxiously. "We got them to go the right way again, but then they started running."

"All you can do when that happens is wait for them to get tired. Look, they're slowing down."

Huffing, the herd was shuffling to a walk.

Kirsty sighed, relieved.

I tried my best, she reminded herself, preparing her defence. *Of course I'm going to make mistakes; I'm learning on the job.*

"That darn Freckle Face. I don't know why the old folks don't get rid of her. She's more trouble than she's worth." He leaned down from Quincy's saddle and patted Lancelot's neck. "You finally figured out what you're supposed to do, hey, Patches?"

"Lancelot," Kirsty reminded him. She was surprised he wasn't more upset about the cows running off.

"Well, let's hope old Freckle Face doesn't give us any more trouble," he went on, "but most likely she will."

"Jesse, you know I really haven't done anything like this ever before," ventured Kirsty. "If you just tell me what to do ahead of time, then I can be ready."

He didn't say anything for a long time. Kirsty began to think he'd ignored her question.

"The thing is, there's so much that can happen I don't

even know where to begin. You already know the important stuff—don't spook the cows, don't run the cows, and keep them going the direction you want them going. The rest is just experience. You have to be ready for anything."

"Well, that helps a lot," sighed Kirsty.

Jesse shrugged. "That's just the way it is."

Freckle Face and her calf made two more escape attempts that Jesse easily cut off. But at the fork in the road, they got away completely, doubling back to head up the smaller fork.

"Keep them moving. I'll catch up," Jesse shouted over his shoulder before vanishing over a rise.

"No, Jesse, wait! Come back!" Kirsty called after him, standing in her stirrups. "What if something happens? What am I supposed to do?"

When he didn't return, she sat back down. "Well, Lancelot, looks like it's up to you and me. We're just going to have to do our best, and what we don't know we'll have to fake. Come on, cows, get up there." She copied Jesse's shrill whistle, and the cows and calves resumed their leisurely stroll down the main fork.

The cattle didn't seem to be bothered at all by Jesse's absence. After a few minutes of riding on high alert, tensing at every swipe of a tail or shaking head that might be the first signal of a breakaway, Kirsty relaxed. Lulled by the sway of her pony's walk, she let her thoughts meander along with the cattle. She wondered what Faye was doing right now at the horse show in Alberta. Warming up a horse before a class? Maybe she was competing at this very moment, jumping over enormous obstacles before a grandstand full of spectators. "Good luck, Faye," she whispered, just in case.

She held herself ready, waiting for the familiar pinch. It didn't come.

For the first time since Faye had begun riding Laurence Devries' string of talented show jumpers, Kirsty didn't feel left out.

Right now she wasn't behind the scenes on the farm, filling in for Faye and practising every spare moment, trying to catch up, knowing it could take years and even then she might never reach her extraordinarily gifted friend's level of riding. She and Lancelot were doing something useful, something necessary, and doing okay. This time when Faye returned from a horse show, Kirsty would have her own stories to tell.

She began to rehearse them in her head. She imagined Faye's face, round eyed with awe, as she listened intently to every word of Kirsty's tales of adventure and drama on a mountain cattle drive. Hemmed in by the trees, the cattle kept in formation, plodding down the dirt road, while Lancelot ambled after them on a loose rein. Kirsty was soon completely caught up in the creation of a dramatic saga, all the right words flowing into place, the tension building to a fever pitch at the very end...

Her stomach rumbled. She sat up in the saddle, blinking as if she'd just woken up. Her belly growled again, demanding to be fed. She looked up and saw a glint of the sun above the trees. The treetops swayed slightly, a hot wind blowing through them. Once again she thought she could detect a faint odour of smoke.

Another complaint from her stomach. It must be close to noon, or was she just hungry from getting up so early? Without a watch she couldn't be sure. She switched the reins to her right hand and reached back with the other to tug open the buckle on the left saddlebag. She pulled out the sandwiches Midge had given her, removed the plastic wrapping and took a bite. Roast beef on homemade brown bread. She'd never tasted anything so good.

The sandwiches disappeared quickly. She changed her reins back to her other hand and fumbled at the strap on the right saddlebag. It opened with an ease that surprised her. She looked back and saw the buckle was gone. She delved into the canvas pocket and found a single water bottle. The second bottle must have fallen out when Lancelot had bolted.

She poured half the water down her throat and started to twist the cap back on the bottle. She was still desperately thirsty. Recklessly, she unscrewed the cap and gulped the rest of the bottle. Jesse could share his water with her, she told herself as she stowed the empty bottle in the saddle-bag. After all, it was his fault she'd lost her second bottle.

But where *was* Jesse? She twisted around in her saddle, half expecting to see him sneaking up on her and Lancelot. He wasn't there.

I'll catch up.

Had he meant he'd find her before they met up with the rest of the drive? He hadn't really expected her to be in charge of moving these cows and calves all the way down the mountain, had he?

Not that they were giving her any trouble. Just as Lucy had predicted, the older cows were marching purposefully along. Occasionally, an animal on the fringes of the herd would veer into the woods, only to find the ground was long bare of grass. Pushing through the crackling brush, she would quickly rejoin the other cattle.

The sun was directly overhead now. Jesse had been gone a long time, at least half an hour, maybe even a whole hour. Kirsty tried to convince herself it was all right, he'd show up any second now. She scanned the woods anxiously, her head swivelling back and forth like an owl's, just in case he was up to another one of his stupid practical jokes and would come charging out of the trees at any moment. She pulled up Lancelot and listened intently for the warning crackle of breaking brush.

The herd shuffled on down the road. As they moved away, quiet settled over the forest. Kirsty closed her eyes. She could hear the soft whoosh of her pony's breathing and...nothing else. The silence was complete. Not a squawk or chirp from a bird, no rustle of small creatures in the brush of the forest floor, not even the hum of an insect.

The back of her neck prickled. Around her the forest felt empty. Her fingertips were suddenly cold, and for some reason her heart rate kicked up for a few beats.

"Don't be silly," she whispered out loud to herself. "Everything's okay."

Another breeze whined through the treetops, rattling the dry branches. It died away in a long sigh.

Lancelot spun around to face up the road, holding his head high and whinnying.

"What is it, boy?" She stood up in her stirrups, trying to see past a bend in the road. "Jesse! Jesse, are you there?"

Her voice echoed through the trees and fell away. There was no answering shout. Lancelot's ribs vibrated as he whinnied again.

Hoofbeats thundered on the road above them, growing louder and louder. Relieved, Kirsty tightened her reins, preparing to get out of the way.

Quincy burst around the bend, reins dangling from his bridle.

His saddle was empty.

4

"Jesse!" Kirsty shouted. "Jesse! Yell if you can hear me!"

She held her breath, listening hard. She heard nothing.

"If this is another one of your jokes, it's not funny." She turned around slowly, ready for him to pop out from behind a tree. "Lancelot, is he out there somewhere?"

The pony's ears were tuned to Quincy. Kirsty waited some more, but nothing else attracted Lancelot's attention. She stepped down out of the saddle and went after Quincy.

The big quarter horse rooted through the brush beside the road, searching for grass. He rolled an eye as she approached on foot but didn't move until she bent down to pick up his trailing reins. As her fingers were about to close around the thin strap of leather, he ducked away, flinging his head high, and trotted off after the herd.

"Come on, Quincy, cut it out." Kirsty followed after him, but each time he spun away just as she was about to grab the reins. After three more tries she swung up on Lancelot, thinking she might be able to get close enough on horse-back, but as soon as she came up beside him the cagey old horse darted away. "Jesse, I can't catch your horse," Kirsty yelled. "You'd better come and get him before he steps on his reins or something."

She scanned the trees, expecting Jesse to slink out from behind one. He didn't.

"Well, let's try again," Kirsty said to her pony, annoyed.

As soon as they caught up with him, Quincy darted and dodged through the herd, shouldering cows aside to escape his pursuers. He reached the front of the herd and sprinted past the leaders, delivering a few sharp nips on the way. Startled, the lead cows broke into a trot. The cattle Quincy had pushed out of the way milled around, shoving other cows out of their places in the herd.

Quincy pranced at the head of the herd, head tossing and tail flagging, his reins flapping like streamers.

A rolling-eyed cow drew up alongside him. He reached over and bit her shoulder. The cow broke into a clumsy canter. Quincy nipped her again.

"Quincy, stop that," Kirsty shouted. Defiantly, the big horse sank his teeth into the cow's rump.

Bawling, the frightened cow began to run. Within seconds, the entire herd thundered after her.

Kirsty grabbed for the saddle horn as Lancelot plunged after Quincy and the herd, charging recklessly down the mountain road. "Help! Jesse, help me! Jesse!"

The stampede swerved unchecked around a switchback.

As Lancelot galloped flat out downhill at the back of the herd, Kirsty squealed in panic, her cries lost beneath the bellowing and hollering of the frightened cows. She clung with both hands to the saddle horn, fingernails digging into the stout leather, feet slipping out of the stirrups.

"Stop! Whoa! Lancelot, whoa!"

In desperation, she removed her hand from the horn and pulled hard on the reins. Lancelot shook his head against the pressure of the bit, but Kirsty didn't let go. His stride slowed, lurching to a rough trot and then finally to a prancing halt.

"Whoa! Lancelot, I mean it. Stand still!"

He shook his head, hopping on his front end like a rabbit. Kirsty had the reins so tight his chin was nearly touching his chest, but he wouldn't stop jumping about.

She managed to get him turned around. She eased off the reins and tapped him with her heels. When the pony balked and pinned his ears, Kirsty reached back and swatted his rump. "Enough of that. You get up now, you hear? We've got to find Jesse."

If turning Quincy loose was another one of Jesse's stupid jokes, it had gone terribly wrong.

And if it wasn't...that was even worse.

Lancelot shuffled reluctantly up the road. Kirsty still hoped to meet up with Jesse making his way down the road on foot. When they climbed switchback after switchback and there was still no sign of him, she began to get edgy.

Where was the fork in the road? She didn't recall its being this far along. She'd just about made up her mind to turn back and go for help when the pony abruptly swerved to the side of the road.

There it was, the fork Jesse and Quincy had taken in pursuit of the renegade cow Freckle Face.

"Jesse! Jesse, can you hear me?"

Still no answer.

She clucked to her pony and sent him onto the new road. His sulkiness fell away and he stepped out eagerly.

After rising up for a way, the fork road dropped down to end abruptly at the edge of a gully. Trees and brush were packed close together in the narrow canyon, but Lancelot found a winding path and took her down it. He was always alert on the trails, but now he was travelling with an unfamiliar wariness, his wide ears turning constantly, his head held higher than usual. Kirsty took the reins in one hand, western style, and let the other hand settle over the saddle horn, ready to hold hard if the pony suddenly spooked.

It was blessedly cool in the gully, with a light breeze rattling dry leaves. Kirsty looked around for signs that Quincy and Jesse had come this way, but she couldn't make out any clues. Powdery dust covered the trail, too thin and wispy to hold any tracks.

Lancelot picked his way over fallen trees. Brush snapped and cracked as he pushed his way through. He stepped across a long-dry stream bed. The moss on the rocks was rough and bristled. He dropped his head and sniffed at the rocks. To Kirsty's dismay he changed direction to follow the dry bed. Just before it slanted uphill, where the brush and trees were thick and green, he began to paw at a patch of gravel with one front foot.

"Lancelot, stop that! What are you doing?"

He wouldn't quit even with her kicking her heels at his belly. His hoof was acting like a shovel, digging a hole that was soon as deep as his fetlock.

"Hey, are you okay?"

Maybe he was starting to colic—pawing was one of the signs. Kirsty ran through the other symptoms Lucy had told her about. Stamping the hind feet, tail swishing, sweating, looking around at the flanks where the bellyache would be lodged. Lancelot was doing none of those things.

Then suddenly he stopped. He lowered his head, snuffling at the hole he'd made. Moments later she heard the unmistakable slurp of drinking.

Lancelot had found water.

"How did you do that?" Kirsty slipped from the saddle. She realized with a pang of remorse that she hadn't even thought of sharing her water with her pony. "Oh, Lancelot, I'm so sorry."

Lancelot flicked his ears at her apology and waited patiently for his shallow water hole to fill before drinking another mouthful. He lifted his head, a few drops dribbling over his fuzzy lips, and sighed.

Slowly water seeped through the gravel into the hole. Kirsty knelt down to wet her hands and wrists and swipe them over her face, washing away the trail dust. She soaked her bandana and squeezed water down the back of her neck. She dipped the bandana into the water hole again and pressed it to her face, her head bowed in relief.

Her mouth and throat were parched, but she didn't know if the water was safe for a person to drink. Resolutely, she got to her feet and stood aside while Lancelot drank again. Then she got back on and gave the pony his head.

Lancelot threaded a path through the heavy brush to the far side of the gully. Kirsty couldn't make out any trail, but Lancelot seemed to know where he was going. He clambered up the far side, zigging and zagging around seedling poplars and cedars. Kirsty leaned forward in her stirrups to balance her weight over his shoulders. At the top he stopped to catch his breath.

Up here the trees were spaced farther apart, the heat weighing down in between them. Away from the shelter of the gully the breeze was warm and strong, blowing about heated air like a furnace vent. Lancelot heaved a long breath and started off again, following a barely visible path winding through the forest, dead grass and underbrush crunching under his feet like potato chips. Every so often Kirsty pulled him up and called Jesse's name, then listened intently for a reply, but she heard nothing.

The trail broke in two. Lancelot didn't pause, just turned onto the upward path and began to climb.

"I hope you know where we're going, Ponyboy," she said, "because I sure don't."

She scanned the trees and bushes surrounding them, trying to pick out landmarks. The forest crowded around them, blocking her view in all directions but straight overhead. She found herself hoping with each turn that the trail would open up onto a meadow or a clearing—any break in the endless ranks of trees standing rigidly like soldiers. A sense of being hemmed in, trapped between the unyielding rough-barked trunks, began to build in her.

They're just trees, she told herself sternly. *They can't move or think.*

But they were alive. She could sense their presence, solid and steadfast around her. They seemed aware of her and Lancelot too, passing through their midst.

The trail climbed up, as steep as a flight of stairs. She leaned onto her pony's neck as he hiked uphill. It began to seem more and more unlikely that Jesse had ridden Quincy after Freckle Face over such rugged terrain. She was a cow, not a mountain goat: maybe she had doubled back to the split to continue downhill on the easier path. But then wouldn't Kirsty have met up with her? Lancelot was scrambling bent legged up the mountainside. As soon as he reached a good place to rest, some patch of level ground, she'd pull him up, rest him until he'd caught his breath and then turn around.

She knew she'd made a mistake. When Quincy had come back without Jesse, she should have gone for help right away instead of going to look for him. But Jesse had fooled her once and made her feel silly—she'd wanted to be sure he wasn't playing another trick on her. Now she realized that even Jesse would not leave himself stranded this far out in the bush, not by choice.

What chance was there that she'd find him in all this wilderness? A lone boy among all these trees—it was a nearly impossible task. It would take a search party to locate him, and then it might be too late. Even now Jesse could be lying hurt, broken limbed, maybe even bleeding and unconscious, and in need of immediate rescue.

She'd made the wrong choice.

She was anxious to go back, but the trail was crossing a rock slide, Lancelot picking his way with great care across the brittle shale. The rocks under his hind feet fell away, rattling down over the scree. His back hooves pedalled, slipping on loose rocks until somehow he found stable footing.

Kirsty let out her breath. She reached down and

cautiously patted his neck, careful not to throw off his balance. She didn't dare risk asking him to turn around, not right here.

As soon as the pony's four feet were on solid ground again, she pulled him up. He dropped his head, breathing hard, his sides rising and falling under her legs. She wanted to get down and relieve him of the burden of her weight, but the trail was so narrow there was nowhere for her to stand.

They were on a shoulder of the mountainside beneath a shallow cliff, the trail going around a bend to yet another ravine wrinkled into the face of the mountain. Back down at the ranch, the mountain range had seemed to be a single row marching against the skyline, but now Kirsty could see that crowded back in behind were peaks and ridges as far as the eye could see, all heavily carpeted with dark green conifers. Deep navy blue shadows blurred the outlines of the farthest ranges, so it was hard to discern where the mountains ended and the sky began.

Lancelot's head jerked up, his nostrils flaring to scent the air. A tremor ran through him. Kirsty followed his ears as they scanned the forest. They held still, and a moment later she heard branches snapping. Three shadows loped through the trees. The larger shadow at the back reared up, her broad black snout pointed in their direction. Before Kirsty could react, the mama bear dropped down and hustled her cubs away.

More branches cracked, and Lancelot jumped in his tracks. Kirsty blinked in surprise as Freckle Face and her calf blundered through the bush in the wake of the bear and cubs. Her mind couldn't take in what she'd just seen—a cow and calf following a mother bear and her cubs? Where were they all going?

The important thing was the cow had come this way and so, Kirsty hoped, had Jesse. This had to be the right trail after all. She clucked to Lancelot to start him moving along.

"Jesse! Where are you? Call if you can hear me!"

A shower of rocks tumbled over the edge of the cliff. Lancelot swung around, his hind end perched precariously off the trail, then steadied himself so he was facing back the way they had come. More rocks bounced down around them, followed by a spray of dirt. The pony skittered back.

"Whoa, steady now."

A pair of bare feet slid into view on the cliff above.

Kirsty stared up at the motionless feet.

"Jesse," she whispered, horrified. "Oh, no, Jesse."

And then she screamed.

5

"Kirsty! Kirsty, what's wrong?"

The bare feet were gone. Now Jesse's head and shoulders stuck out from the cliff.

Jesse's talking head.

"Jesse! You're alive! What happened? Are you all right?"

He shrugged. "Yeah, I'm okay."

"Are you sure? You're not hurt?"

"I'm fine. Got it?" For someone who'd just been rescued he didn't seem very happy...or grateful.

"I can't believe we found you. We've been looking and looking. Quincy came back without you and—"

"Where's my horse?"

"I couldn't catch him. He wouldn't let me get near. And then he started chasing the cows and...well, he ran away with them."

"Why didn't you stop him?"

"I tried!"

"This is great, just great. The grandfolks are really going to be impressed with me now. Another screw-up, the story of my life. I must be jinxed."

"Jesse, what happened?"

He swung his legs around so he was sitting up, his bare feet dangling over the edge. Kirsty waited, but he didn't answer her question.

"Did you get bucked off?" she persisted.

"No!" he snarled.

"You're not injured at all? Not even a broken toenail?"

He rolled his eyes to the sky and slowly shook his head.

"Okay, so where are your boots?"

"Back there." He jerked his head over his shoulder.

Kirsty gritted her teeth. "Why aren't they on your feet?"

"Because I took them off. Look, I don't want to talk about it, okay?" His face was red.

"All right, then, Jesse, if that's the way you want it." Kirsty clucked to Lancelot.

"Where are you going? Kirsty, stop! Hey, you can't just go off and leave me!"

"Jesse Sims, you've been nothing but rude and nasty to me from the moment we met. I don't know why and I don't care! All I know is I'm not putting up with it anymore. So don't expect me to help you."

"But I don't even have my boots!"

"That's your problem, not mine."

"Okay, okay, I'm sorry. Kirsty, don't go. Please come back."

She didn't. As Lancelot stepped off the scree onto solid ground again, Kirsty found she was shaking, her blood pounding in her ears. She'd never been so furious with someone in her life.

She hurried her pony down the trail. At the moment all she wanted was to get far away from Jesse.

By the time they re-entered the gully, her anger was cooling. *Now what?* she asked herself as Lancelot drank from the water hole.

Stepping off her pony she hunkered down in the shade and thought about the situation. She didn't look forward to riding back down the mountain all by herself. And then, if she did manage to find her way to Lucy and the other riders, they were certainly going to notice she'd returned without her partner. Of course, they'd want to know why. How could she explain leaving Jesse alone in the wilderness without his horse or even his boots?

And what would he say about her, once he'd been rescued? It was no good thinking his grandparents and the others would ride off home to the ranch and leave him behind; they'd start searching for him right away when they learned he was missing, just like she had.

She didn't have to ponder long to realize what she had to do.

Jesse was still sitting on the cliff edge when she returned.

"Okay, let's get your boots," she said.

"I got off somewhere along here," Jesse said. He was sitting behind Kirsty on the skirt of the saddle. Since she'd come back, he'd been very quiet, except for giving out directions.

Kirsty studied the thick brush lining the thin rivulet that trickled through the gully folded into the mountainside. She judged they were in the same gully she and Lancelot had gone through earlier, a lot farther up the mountain at a point where the narrow stream was still above ground. Lancelot carefully descended to the base of the gully. "You don't remember exactly where?"

"No. I didn't pay close attention. You see, I wasn't thinking about leaving and having to find them again." He slid down off the pony, taking care to keep his bare feet well away from the hooves.

"Jesse, what happened?"

"You're going to keep pestering me until I tell you, aren't you?"

"Probably," Kirsty admitted.

He studied his bare feet for a while. "This is going to sound real stupid. I tracked Freckle Face up here. 'Course the moment I got here, she ran off again. I let her go since she was heading in the right direction. And then, well, it had been a long climb. Quincy needed a rest. So I got off." He paused.

"And then?"

"Well, my feet were cooking in my boots. It seemed like a good idea to pull them off and have a soak in the stream, just for a minute or two. And everything would have been just fine except a moose came crashing through the bush and spooked Quincy real bad. He pulled away from me. I ran after him and almost caught him twice, but then he took off and left me stranded. Until you came along."

He picked his way gingerly through the brushy stream bed. "There they are!"

Kirsty dismounted and led Lancelot to the stream. The banks were quite muddy, but the water flowed through a bed of rock and gravel. While the pony slurped at the water, she wet her face. She stared at the brown-tinged water doubtfully.

Re-booted, Jesse took the pony's reins from her. "You can have a drink. It's flowing through gravel; that purifies it."

She picked her way upstream and hunkered down. She scrubbed her hands and then cupped them together to scoop the water to her mouth. She closed her eyes and savoured the relief of water sliding down her parched throat.

When she returned, Jesse was rubbing at the drying sweat on Lancelot's neck and chest with a fistful of scrunched brush and twigs. The pony's eyes were nearly closed in bliss.

"Feels good, doesn't it, Patches? You're a good fellow."

Jesse glanced over his shoulder at the sound of Kirsty's footsteps. "Hey, listen, I…well, I want to say thank you. For coming looking for me."

"I couldn't just leave you behind."

"A lot of people would have," said Jesse darkly.

"No, they wouldn't. People are better than that."

"That's what you think. I know different."

"So now what do we do?"

"Head down the mountain, like we were doing before. The cows probably didn't run long. If we're lucky we'll find them, and Quincy, too. Gather them up again, get them down the mountain and everything will be fine."

"And if we don't?"

"Well, then I'm in a lot of trouble…again. Who knows what they'll do to me this time."

"What do you mean?" Kirsty had just asked when Lancelot flung his head, nostrils flaring. She sniffed the air. "Do you smell that?"

Jesse shut his eyes and breathed in. "Smoke. The wind's changed; it's blowing this way."

"But the fire's back in the mountains, a long way from here, right?"

"It was." His eyes studied the sky anxiously.

Kirsty tipped her head back to look up. She squinted at the faint haze drifting across the blue and sighed in relief. Finally, clouds. She watched the thickening mist closely, praying fat-bellied rain clouds would be right behind.

Instead the mist was settling onto the treetops, sinking lower and lower into the gully. As it thickened, the acrid stench of wood ash filled the air.

Kirsty felt her heartbeat quicken. This was no mist.

"Get on," said Jesse. "Right now. Hurry, Kirsty."

Her foot fumbled for the stirrup. Even as she was swinging aboard, Jesse had turned the pony. "Hang on!" He smacked Lancelot on the rump.

The pony plunged up the side of the gully. "Jesse! Where are you?"

Lancelot lurched and scrambled up the steep path. Kirsty cried out as the saddle horn hit her in the ribs. She tried to look around for Jesse, but it was all she could do to stay in the saddle.

She opened her mouth to call for him again and choked on a lungful of smoke.

Lancelot broke over the top of the gully. Kirsty pulled him up.

She looked back and there was Jesse, hanging on to the pony's tail with both hands like a tow rope. Her eyes widened as she looked over his head. Jesse dropped the tail and turned around. They both stared at the scene before them, transfixed.

Through the trees the air seemed to shimmer. The entire skyline was aglow. Even as they watched, copper, crimson and golden flames reached higher and higher until they melted into the sun.

The forest was on fire.

6

"*Now* why are we stopping?" said Patty, gently braking the truck and horse trailer to a halt. "More construction? Why do they wait for summer to fix the roads?"

Faye hitched forward in the back seat to peer over the groom's shoulder at the long line of cars stopped in front of them. She glanced out the side window. The other lane was completely empty.

In the passenger seat, Laurence Devries let out a long sigh. "How long will this delay be?"

Patty rammed the gearshift into park. "I'm going to see if anyone knows. It's much too hot to keep the horses standing in a parked trailer." She slipped out of the air-conditioned cab and slammed the door shut behind her.

Mr. Devries twisted in his seat and grinned at Faye. "I'm sure Patty will have us underway in no time."

Faye grinned back. "Look, here she comes already."

"Well, did you convince the works crew to let us through?" asked Mr. Devries.

Patty shook her head as she hoisted herself into the cab. "Nobody's getting through. The highway's closed. There's a forest fire in the area."

"Where?"

"Some place called Falkland."

"I know where that is," said Faye. "It must be a big fire for the highway to be closed all the way over here."

Patty expertly turned the truck and horse trailer completely around. "We'll have to go all the way back through Salmon Arm. I don't know how long it's going to take us to get to Hillcroft Farm." She yawned, rolling her shoulders.

"You've been driving all night, Patty. You must be tired. Would you like me to take the wheel?" asked Mr. Devries.

"Thanks, Laurence, but I'm fine. I'm just so annoyed that we had to haul that horse all the way to Kamloops. If those people had kept up a proper maintenance program on their truck, it wouldn't have broken down in Rogers Pass."

"Now, Patty, what were we supposed to do—leave them stranded by the side of the road with a horse in the trailer?"

"Of course not, Laurence. But between that and this road closure, we're going to be very late getting home."

Mr. Devries got out his cell phone and held it over the back of his seat. "Faye, would you like to try calling your grandmother again?"

"Yes, please." No one picked up at the farm. After five rings the answering machine came on. Faye waited impatiently for the beep. "Hi, Grandma and Riley, it's me. Guess what, I'm on my way home. Elan lost a shoe and bruised her foot, so we left early. I'll explain everything when I get there. We'll be there in..."

"An hour?" Patty supplied. "Maybe an hour and a half?"

"An hour or so," Faye continued. "We have to go the long way around because there's a forest fire in Falkland. See you soon. Love you." She ended the call and wondered if she should ask to phone Kirsty and tell her to come to the farm, if she wasn't there already. After nearly a month on the road, Faye had a lot to tell her best friend.

"And now I must call my dear sister and tell her not to expect me for lunch after all." Mr. Devries held out his hand for the phone. "She doesn't like it when plans are changed at short notice."

After he had endured his sister's scolding, he turned on the radio.

"...jumped the highway and is burning out of control. Emergency evacuations of residents and livestock are underway."

"That sounds serious," said Mr. Devries. "Faye, how far is Falkland from your farm?"

"Oh, it's a long way."

"So we don't have to worry about Lucy and your friend Kirsty."

"Those poor people," said Patty. "Can you imagine having to move all your livestock at short notice? Where would you take them? How would you get them there?"

"A nightmare," said Mr. Devries. "It's an absolute nightmare."

"What day is it today?" asked Faye anxiously. At the horse show, focused completely on each day's competitions, she'd lost track of time.

"Monday," Patty told her.

"Oh, no."

"What is it, Faye?" asked Mr. Devries.

"My grandma—last time I phoned she told me she was going on a cattle drive at a ranch near Falkland. I can't remember if she said Sunday or Monday."

"Is there anyone you can call to find out? What about your brother?" Mr. Devries held out his phone again.

"Riley! He'll know!" She punched in her brother's cell number. "No answer."

"Maybe he's in an area with no service," suggested Patty.

"He does turn off his phone when he's at work." Faye's eyes met Patty's in the rear-view mirror.

"Don't worry," Patty said. "I'm sure everything's fine."

"That's right," seconded Mr. Devries. "Perhaps your grandmother has gone into town to do some errands."

"That's probably where she is," agreed Faye. "Getting groceries. Or at the bank. Or…something."

She slid back in her seat. She closed her eyes, took a

couple of long, deep breaths and imagined her worry as a channel on television. Deliberately she switched the channel to replays of her jumping rounds. Here she was on Elan approaching the first fence in what was to be their winning performance. Stretch tall, tighten her legs and up, up, up and over.

"The truck and horse trailer are gone. So are Blackbird and Lancelot. Kirsty must be with my grandma," Faye said as she came down the alley of the barn. "And Stubby was locked in the tack room." A short-legged terrier waddled out the barn door to inspect the truck tires.

Patty and Mr. Devries looked at each other before they turned to her.

"Well, maybe they hauled out to go trail riding somewhere," said Patty. She moved the water hose to Elan's bucket.

"They'd go up the mountain behind the farm for a trail ride."

"Perhaps they wanted to go somewhere different."

"They would have taken Stubby. He rides on the front of the saddle with my grandma."

"She probably decided he'd be better off at home. This heat can kill dogs, you know. They don't sweat like horses or people do."

"I knew that," Faye muttered to herself as she cut the

strings on a bale of hay and divvied it up into flakes. She tossed a couple of flakes into Ebon's and Erol's stalls. The horses would be staying at Hillcroft Farm before leaving for the next competition.

Patty looked around from turning off the water. "Oh, Faye, hold on a moment. I want to weigh that hay to make sure they're getting the right amount."

Faye clicked her tongue in annoyance. She'd been feeding horses and ponies for years and could judge the weight of a flake of hay just by holding it in her hands.

Elan nickered, pawing with her front hoof as Faye stood in front of her stall with the black mare's hay. Patty bustled up with her scale and took the hay.

"Be patient, pretty girl. I know it's hard to wait, but we have to be patient." Faye ran her hand under the mare's jowls and gently scratched the velvet skin. Elan stretched her neck, her upper lip quivering in bliss. Even like this, with her ears lopping out at the sides of her head, her eyes half closed and her top lip curled down like a camel's, she was the most beautiful horse Faye had ever seen. Faye marvelled again that not only was she allowed to ride her, but she was even getting paid for it.

Patty pulled a sliver of hay from the bale to add to Elan's meal and set it in the mare's stall. "There we go." She fussed around the mare, tugging her fly sheet into place, smoothing her mane. "Now, are you sure you're going to be able to poultice that foot? I'm worried it could become abscessed. Maybe I should just stay and give you a hand. I could set up a cot in the tack room."

"Patty, you are taking a few days off," said Mr. Devries firmly. "Faye and Lucy will give the horses excellent care. Now, Faye, have you checked at the house for a message from your grandmother?"

"I'll do that right now."

There was nothing.

"This is where we leave messages for each other," said Faye, standing by the blank whiteboard next to the telephone with Stubby in her arms.

"Well, she didn't know you were coming home early from the horse show, so why would she leave a message?" said Patty.

"I wanted to surprise her and Riley. Now I wish I'd called and told them."

"Is this where Lucy would have left a message for your brother?" asked Mr. Devries.

"Yes, but there's nothing for him either…oh, so he must have known ahead of time that she and Kirsty were going somewhere."

"Exactly. Call Riley again."

Still no answer.

"Try him at work," Patty said.

"That's just it—I don't know where he works. He quit

at Arnold's Burgers and started at some hotel in Vernon. I didn't pay attention when he told me the name."

Suddenly Stubby catapulted from her arms and bolted, yapping, out the screen door.

"Someone's here," said Mr. Devries.

A car door slammed and someone stomped up the steps onto the veranda. "Lucy? Are you in there?" The door flung open and a woman stuck her frizzy head inside. "Who are you people?"

Faye moved into view. "It's me, Mrs. Finney. This is Laurence Devries and Patty McGill."

"Where's your grandmother? I've been phoning her all morning."

"I don't know. We just got in from Alberta. Is something wrong?"

"So you haven't heard about the fire."

"We did hear something on the radio," said Mr. Devries. "It's in Falkland and the highway is closed."

"It's a heck of a lot closer than Falkland! It came across the highway and over the mountain onto Yankee Flats. With this wind there's no stopping it. Is that your rig outside?"

"Yes, it is."

"They're calling for anyone with a truck and trailer to move livestock out of there. That's why I was phoning Lucy, to see if she could help. How about you?"

"Certainly," said Mr. Devries. "Where do we go?"

"Got a pencil and paper? I'll draw you a map. How many horses can you take in here?" Mrs. Finney looked up from her map drawing at Faye.

"I don't know. I'd have to check with my grandmother first."

"There's no time. We need more stalls and corrals. They're taking animals to the fairgrounds in town right now, but it's filling up fast."

"Then of course they must bring some here. It's okay, Faye, I'll take responsibility for this decision," said Mr. Devries. "Could you fill a few water bottles for us so we have something to drink?"

As Faye turned on the tap, she overheard him saying to Mrs. Finney, "...might be on a cattle drive somewhere up that mountain." She looked around just in time to see Mrs. Finney clap her hand over her mouth. Faye left the water running and moved closer, pretending to search the cupboard for another water bottle.

"I'll let the emergency response coordinators know. Oh my goodness, I hope they're safe."

"We'll pray that they are. Ah, all ready, Faye?"

She nodded.

"Then we're on our way."

Kirsty stared, mesmerized by the pulsing horizon of gold and orange. She squeezed her eyes shut and opened them again, hardly able to believe what she was seeing.

There was a heavy, dull feeling at the bottom of her stomach. A tear dripped onto her cheek, and she realized she was trembling all over.

Then Lancelot was spinning around as Jesse pulled at his reins. "Get out of here!" He slapped the pony's rump. "Boot him, Kirsty! Get going!"

"Jesse, no! Not without you!"

Lancelot was half rearing, fighting against Kirsty's stranglehold on the reins.

"I mean it, Jesse, we're not leaving you. Get on!"

"I'll slow you down."

"We're getting out of this together, or..." She didn't bother finishing the sentence.

Jesse vaulted aboard. Kirsty let the pony go.

"Come on, Lancelot, go, go, go!"

Lancelot ignored the path and plunged straight down

the mountainside, ducking and diving around trees. Kirsty clung to the saddle horn with both hands, jouncing from side to side as the pony stumbled over rocks and plowed through bushes. Branches smacked Kirsty's face and arms; wild rose thorns clawed her skin. Behind her Jesse squawked as the branches and thorns had their turn at him.

Lancelot tripped over a fallen log and stumbled to his knees. Kirsty flopped onto his neck like a rag doll, gasping as the saddle horn punched the air out of her. The pony staggered to his feet and lurched forward.

Hunched over the horn, Kirsty looked up. The tree branch was right there, too close to avoid. It caught her right across the collarbones as Lancelot pushed under it, breaking loose her handhold and shoving her over the back of the saddle into Jesse. Her feet flew up and she somersaulted over the pony's haunches into a thicket of willow.

She lay tangled on her side in the willow branches, whooping for air as Lancelot vanished into the trees.

"Kirsty! Are you all right? Come on, say something."

Jesse was a few feet away, lying on his back with his knees bent. He rolled onto his knees and crawled over, his face just a few inches from hers.

"What's the matter? Please, will you just speak?"

"Can't...breathe."

"Okay, stay calm. The wind's been knocked out of you. Just relax, let the air back into your lungs. Is it getting better?"

Kirsty nodded. It was getting easier to breathe, little by little.

Jesse banged his fist into his forehead. "What a mess! Now we're going to have to walk out of here."

"Lancelot will come back," croaked Kirsty.

"This is all my fault. If I hadn't taken off my boots and Quincy hadn't run off, none of this would have happened. What was I thinking? Dad's right; I'm a real screw-up." Now he was thumping the ground with his fist.

The pressure on Kirsty's chest suddenly eased and her lungs refilled with air. "Oh, stop feeling so sorry for yourself. Come on, help me get out of this bush."

Jesse caught her wrists and tugged her out. He yanked a twig out of her hair. "You're a real mess."

"Thanks, Jesse, that makes me feel real good right now."

"Oh, great, now you're crying."

"I'm not crying." Impatiently, Kirsty knuckled away her tears.

"Yes, you are."

"So what if I am? We're lost in the mountains with a forest fire right behind us!"

"We're not lost. I've got a good idea where we are. Come on, we've got to get going."

"Wait, Lancelot's not back yet."

"Kirsty, your pony isn't coming back here. He's an animal. Right now, he's running to save his skin."

"You go. I'm not leaving without Lancelot."

"You're a real pain, you know that?"

"And you're a bigger pain, *you* know that?"

Branches snapped behind them. Jesse scooped up a rock.

Twigs skewered in his bushy mane, Lancelot squirmed through a thicket and walked up to them.

"See, told you." Kirsty couldn't resist.

"Unreal," said Jesse.

They remounted and continued down the mountain. The trail abruptly snaked back toward the rock slide and the gully beyond.

Lancelot carefully picked his way back across the scree. Kirsty looked up, but the cliff above them blocked out any view of the fire.

Jesse shifted impatiently behind her. "Come on, pony, hurry up. We've got to get to the main road."

Lancelot stepped onto firm ground again and began to jog. The trees thickened, hiding the fire behind them. Overhead, charcoal-grey puffs of smoke billowed across the sky.

The pony's neck dipped, and they were jouncing down the steep slope into the gully. Willow branches slapped their shins and thighs as Lancelot forced his way through. And then he was hiking bent kneed up the far side.

Kirsty clung to a hank of mane and tried to recall how

much farther it was to the main road. A long way yet, most of it slow going over rough terrain. And straight across the mountain, too, not down, the direction all her instincts were urging her to go.

Lancelot staggered over the edge of the gully. He halted, trembling underneath his riders.

"Oh," said Jesse. His voice was filled with awe and fear.

They were on a small knoll, looking out over the forest. Rivers of amber and scarlet flames threaded across the mountain slopes before them. A crest of golden fire followed the skyline, topped with swirling clouds of grey smoke. As they stared, the smoke clouds began to glow, ruby and vermilion tongues of flames flickering in their bellies.

In the short time they'd been down in the gully, the fire had staked claim on the mountain.

A strange chill washed through Kirsty, right down to the pit of her stomach. Fear. She was shaking, her teeth chattering.

Lancelot swung around back down into the gully. Instead of going back up the other side, he forced a path through the brush at the bottom.

"Let him go! Let him go!" said Jesse when Kirsty tried to steer the pony out of the gully floor.

With no trail to follow and hampered by the thick brush, they made slow progress. When Lancelot stumbled over a fallen log, Jesse slid off his back.

"I'll walk out in front and clear a path."

The gully suddenly angled down. Bare rock poked through the earth to make a crude giant's staircase. Kirsty caught her breath as Lancelot slipped between steps in the loose dirt. The pony caught his balance and stood still, legs shaking.

"You okay?" asked Jesse.

She nodded. "He's tired. He needs to rest."

"Just for a few moments. We've got to keep going."

"Jesse, what about the others? Your grandparents and Lucy—will they be all right?"

"They're close to the road. They should be able to get off the mountain pretty quick. I just hope…"

"What? What is it?"

"We've been gone a long time, a lot longer than we should have. We're way overdue to meet up with them. I just hope they haven't come looking for us."

"But if they have, they'll be heading right into the fire!"

Jesse rubbed his hand over his face. "That's what I'm worried about."

"We've got to do something!"

"What, Kirsty, what can we do?"

"This is all your fault! If you hadn't gone off to soak your feet, we would have been on time. Now people could be in real danger, and it's all because of you!"

He hung his head. "I know. Believe me, I know, and I'm sorrier than you can imagine." He turned around and pushed back into the bush.

Hours later—two or three, Kirsty couldn't tell—they were still surrounded on all sides by trees and still slowly going down. The gully had widened into a steep slope. They'd made their way around fallen logs, under low-hanging branches and, once, through a dry creek bed. Lancelot had paused to sniff the rocks and gravel and gone right on.

Kirsty's tongue was dry and clumsy in her mouth. Sweat prickled constantly at her neck and forehead. The sun had dipped in the sky behind the treetops, lowering the temperature a few blessed degrees.

For some time now the air had been clear of smoke. The fire was consuming the forest above them, gorging itself on the thick stands of upland timber.

"We should have reached the road by now." She said aloud the words that had been running through her head for some time. It was the first time she'd spoken since her outburst at Jesse earlier.

"I know," said Jesse.

"Are we lost?"

"I think so."

"Me, too. What do we do?"

"Just keep heading downhill. That's all we can do. This mountain can't go on forever. Sooner or later we're going to come out at the bottom."

"Where will we be then? Will we be on the flats, where the ranch is?"

"I can't say for sure. Kirsty, if you've got any better ideas…"

"No, Jesse, I don't." She remembered the view she'd seen earlier, of mountains running into mountains as far as the eye could see. What if they were going deeper into the mountains instead of toward the valley? Trapped among the trees, surrounded and crowded by brown-barked trunks on every side, she found it impossible to get her bearings. Even the sun overhead was no help, so densely shrouded by a canopy of evergreen branches that it was impossible to pinpoint its location in the sky.

A narrow deer trail crossed their path.

"It's got to go somewhere," said Kirsty. "Let's follow it."

On his own Lancelot turned right onto the trail.

"Not that direction," said Jesse. "Turn him around."

Lancelot shook his head, refusing to go down the left trail.

"Come on, Lancelot, this is no time to be stubborn," said Jesse. He swatted the pony with his hand.

"He wants to go the other way."

"But it goes straight up. We want to get *down* the mountain, so we've got to go this way, to the left."

Kirsty drummed her heels against the pony. "Come on, don't be so difficult."

Lancelot shuffled reluctantly to the left down the deer trail, his ears pinned in protest.

The trail switched back and forth through the forest, dropping with each turn. With each step down the mountainside, Kirsty's spirits lifted. The trees crowded up to each other, wide-skirted cedars brushing against the stubby-branched firs. The air beneath their dark branches was sweet and cool and blessedly free of the stench of smoke.

The trail dropped sharply, skirting large boulders, then levelled out. Kirsty peered through the trees.

"Jesse, I can see light up ahead."

"I can, too. It must be the road!"

"Come on, Lancelot, we're nearly there." She chirped, but the pony had already picked up the pace.

The trees gave way.

"No," groaned Jesse. "No, no, no."

They were at the edge of a rock cliff. Kirsty looked down at the steep slopes of roughly hewn rocks, strewn about the mountainside like the aftermath of a giant toddler's temper tantrum. Stunted shrubs and the occasional skinny tree clung to tiny pockets of dirt between the rocks.

"We're not anywhere near the bottom."

Jesse slipped down from Lancelot. "I'm going to look for a way down."

"No, Jesse," said Kirsty, dismounting. "It's too steep."

His brown head disappeared below the cliff edge. Kirsty loosened the cinch and lifted the saddle up on Lancelot's back to let the air through, the way Lucy had taught her. The pony shook all over, flapping the saddle strings. She settled the saddle back in place. Towing Lancelot along, she explored the clifftop. It ended in a deep cleft of jagged rock, impassable except by mountain goats. She leaned out as far as she dared. The rock cliffs covered this part of the mountainside as far as she could see.

Kirsty retreated, turning around. The mountain rose above her, trees anchored into the steep slope. She peered into their dark shadows, but there was no sign of the deer trail. They were going to have to turn around and retrace their steps.

Playing out the reins to the end, she peered over the cliff. "Jesse? Where are you?"

"Over here." A scraggy bush shook. "I'm on a ledge. Hang on, let's see where it goes. Hmm. Kirsty, how are you with heights?"

"Not very good. I get dizzy on a ladder."

The reins suddenly tightened. Lancelot held his head high, his attention fixed on the trees above them. Kirsty's gut twisted with dread. She followed the pony's gaze and sighed in relief. The sky was clear and blue.

Then, as she watched, a thick white cloud crested the trees, drifting down the mountainside toward the cliff.

"Jesse! We've got to get out of here! We've got to go back!"

The cloud was spreading, a long quilt of fluffy white down floating slowly over the trees. She squinted, detecting a faint glimmer. Abruptly the treetops began to glow, orange and scarlet flames writhing through them.

"Fire," she screeched. "Jesse! It's coming!"

"I'm right here." She saw the top of his brown hair, watched as he grabbed a hunk of long grass to pull himself over the edge. She moved forward to help him.

Out of the corner of her eye she saw the grass handhold flip up, exposing an underside of dry grey dirt. It began to slide. Jesse's eyebrows arched in surprise. His other hand clawed at the rock face. Kirsty dove to her knees, flinging out her hands. She felt Jesse's fingers brush hers, and then he was gone.

Faye drummed her fingers on the armrest as the convoy of trucks and trailers snaked down the switchback.

"I can walk faster than this! Let me out and I'll go up ahead and tell them we need to get through," said Faye as they edged around the final curve at a snail's pace.

"That wouldn't help," said Patty. "*All* these vehicles need to get through."

"The road is closed to regular traffic, Faye," explained Mr. Devries. "Every truck and trailer you see is part of the rescue effort."

Faye squirmed in her seat to look around. There was a long stream of vehicles in front of and behind them. "But there are so many."

"There's a lot of animals to come out," said Patty. "When I spoke to the emergency contact on the phone, he was worried about hauling out all the livestock in time. Some animals might have to be herded out or just turned loose."

"In time?" Faye echoed. "For what?"

"Before the area is cleared, I suppose."

Laurence Devries shot Patty a warning look. "Let's pray everything goes well for all."

Faye slumped back, feeling useless and edgy. Why didn't Lucy have a cell phone, as she'd been urging her? The first thing Faye would do with her share of the prize money they'd won was buy her grandmother one and teach her how to use it.

Phone. Connections sparked in her brain. "Kirsty's mother!"

"Of course," said Mr. Devries. "She'll know where her daughter is. What's the number?" He opened his cell phone and groaned. "No service."

Faye thumped her head against the window.

"Hang in there, kid," said Patty. She jerked her chin at the emergency vehicles at the roadblock ahead. "Help is on the way."

"We must be brave, Faye," said Mr. Devries. "Calm and brave."

Squinting back her tears, Faye pasted a brave look on her face.

"Jesse! Jesse! Answer me!"

Silence.

"Are you okay? Jesse, please say something!"

Kirsty closed her eyes, listening hard. She heard nothing over the dull roar of the approaching inferno. She dropped down onto her stomach and leaned out over the cliff edge as far as she dared. All she could see was rock and shrubs. She inhaled to shout once more and caught her breath. There, she was certain she heard it: a faint groan. "Jesse? Can you hear me?"

A rock rattled down the cliff.

Now silence again. Kirsty wormed back from the cliff edge. She cradled her head in her arms, trying to decide what to do. Jesse was somewhere down the cliff, maybe hurt, or worse—*no, don't think that*. They were lost in the mountains, a forest fire was raging up behind them, and even if she knew in what direction to go looking for help, it was far away.

There was only herself…and her pony. And Lancelot was not a mountain goat. Moving quickly, before she could have second thoughts, she pushed up onto her feet and went to the pony.

"Lancelot, I've got to help Jesse. And you've got to get out of here." She turned him toward the deer trail and pulled the bridle from his head. The pony's wise dark eyes followed her motions. He lowered his head and she pressed her cheek against his bony face, his bushy forelock tickling her face. She inhaled his clean grassy scent, then pulled away. "Get going now. Come on, move it!"

She swung the bridle at his rump. Lancelot startled and jumped away. Kirsty ran at him, whooping and flinging the bridle. The pony shook his head and trotted off toward the trail. She knotted the bridle around her waist like a belt.

Before she could lose her nerve, Kirsty eased herself over the cliff. Lancelot watched her from a distance. "Get out of here!" She pitched a handful of pebbles at him. The pony ducked and vanished up the trail.

"Stay safe, Lancelot. Look after yourself." She swiped her eyes on her forearm and continued to climb down the cliff.

He's going to be all right, she told herself, scraping her foot along the rock face until she found a toehold. *He'll make it. And so will we.*

She glanced down at the sheer wall of rock beneath her. A wave of dizziness spun through her. Quickly she looked away.

"I can't do this," she said out loud. "I need help. Please, someone—anyone—help me. Help! Help! Is anyone out there?"

She was crying, clinging so hard to the rock that her fingers and toes ached.

You have to do this. There is no one but you.

She paused, choking back a sob.

Jesse needs you. Stay calm. Breathe.

The voice inside her was tiny but strong. She forced in a deep breath of air and felt her tears begin to dry.

Just do what you have to do. Don't think about everything right now. Lucy's advice for jumping popped into her head: *Just ride at the fence in front of you. Jump by jump, you'll get around the entire course.*

She stretched down her leg until she felt another bump to set her foot on. She let the rest of her body slide down the rock. Then, slowly, she found another foothold. And another.

The groan caught her by surprise. She'd been so focused, she hadn't realized she was nearly at the bottom. Off to her left, bushes rustled. "Jesse?"

"Kirsty? I'm here. Help me, please."

"Don't move, I'll be right there." She scuttled down onto

a ledge that split open into a shallow crevice. The brush in the crevice rattled, and there were Jesse's boots. Kirsty inched her way along the rock ledge, carefully placing her feet on the bumpy surface. Jesse's knees came into view, tangled among the brush. The ledge was narrower here, not much more than one giant step across, and scattered with loose rocks. Kirsty gingerly slid her feet along it, careful to stay close to the rock face. Finally she was directly above Jesse, looking down into his frightened brown eyes.

"I'm stuck," he said. "I can't get out."

He was wedged into the crevice on his back, his arms trapped against his body by the narrowing rock walls. His legs were free, and as she watched he tried to hook his heels on the sides of the crevice and worm his body along into the wider part of the crack.

"Are you hurt?" asked Kirsty.

He shook his head. "Not badly." He kicked out again and winced. "I might have cracked a couple of ribs. That's nothing, I've done it before playing hockey."

"Your face is really red."

"That's because my feet are higher than my head. Will you please help me?"

She nodded. "I'm just trying to think what to do. You'll have to turn sideways—"

"No! I'll just fall in deeper."

"Okay, okay, take it easy. Stay calm."

"I'm slipping. I can feel it. Pull me out, Kirsty!" He tried to lift his arm.

She hesitated. Even if she lay flat along the ledge, she wouldn't be able to reach him.

"Kirsty, please. Help me."

"I will, Jesse." She looked around for a stick. Lancelot's bridle tugged at her waist. Of course. She pulled it free. "Here, grab this." She swung the reins toward him.

Jesse snatched and missed. "You're still too high."

Sweeping a small area clear of rocks, Kirsty folded herself down onto her knees. She dangled the reins into the crevice. Jesse's fingers stretched up to them. One hand clinging to the ledge, Kirsty leaned out and lowered the bridle.

Jesse grabbed the reins. He pulled hard, heaving up out of the crevice. Kirsty felt herself dragged forward, and for an awful moment she was sure she was going to be pulled in. She braced her shoulders against his weight.

"Pull," Jesse grunted. "Pull!"

"I...am."

His shoulders were free. He was suspended in mid-air, pulling himself up the reins fist over fist.

"I can't hold on!" Kirsty's arms were shaking.

"You can! Just a bit..."

She shook her head, trying to warn him the leather straps were sliding through her damp hands. Her muscles had become rubber.

Jesse slapped a palm onto the ledge. His face twisted with effort.

Kirsty felt an almighty yank on the bridle. She tumbled toward the edge. Jesse's other hand pushed her back.

The second hand was clawing at air. Kirsty grabbed the wrist and pulled it onto the ledge.

Jesse's boots scraped at rock. Kirsty leaned down on the wrist, pinning his upper body onto the ledge.

He had a knee over the edge. Still holding his wrist, she crawled backwards, giving him room. He dragged his foot up. His shoulders twisted as he rolled, pulling up his other leg.

Jesse lay on his side along the ledge, eyes closed, his back to the rock, breathing hard. His shirt was patched with sweat. Kirsty shifted to a sitting position, her arms and shoulders twitching with muscle spasms. She paid them no notice. She rested her head against the rock wall.

She had never felt so alive before. She was so very, very grateful.

Jesse coughed. "Thank you," he croaked.

"You're welcome. Anytime."

"I hope not. This is getting really embarrassing."

"What do you mean?"

"That's the second time you've rescued me. Not good for my image. If the guys ever find out…"

"Don't worry. It will be our secret."

"Just the same, I owe you, Kirsty. If you ever need help, you know who to call, right?"

"Thank you, Jesse." She got up. "Let's just think about getting out of here."

Jesse climbed stiffly to his feet. "Sure thing." He grimaced.

"You *are* hurt."

"Like I said, I must have cracked some ribs. Don't worry, it's happened before. As long as none of them are pushed out of place I'm okay." He winced.

"Why do you have to act like such a tough guy all the time?"

Jesse gave her a strange look. "There are tougher guys than me." He wiped his face on his shirttail. "Come on, we've got to start climbing so we can get Lancelot and get out of here. Kirsty, what's wrong?"

"I turned him loose. When I came to help you. I didn't know what to do...so I let him go." She held up the bridle, tears filling her eyes.

Jesse stared at the bridle. "That's what you used to pull me out." He reached out and ruffled Kirsty's hair. "You did the right thing. He'll be okay. He's one savvy pony. You can tell he knows his way around the bush."

"What do you think he'll do?"

"Most likely he'll head for the ranch. When we get back there, that's where we'll find him, dozing in the shade waiting for you. Quincy will probably be there, too, so he'll have company."

Kirsty held that picture in her mind: Lancelot and Quincy resting under the big willow trees at Mountainridge Ranch.

"I should have listened to that pony earlier," Jesse went on, "instead of making him go the other way."

"What's that noise?"

"I don't hear anything."

"There it is again." Kirsty shut her eyes, listening. "Like some kind of animal howling."

"It's an airplane! Listen, it's louder. It's getting close."

"Is it a water bomber?"

"Maybe. Except—what is it, Kirsty?"

"Something just stung my arm. Look!" She cuffed away a burning ember.

They both looked up.

Overhead the sky flickered and glowed. The howling deepened to a deafening roar that belonged to no living creature or man-made machine. A shower of bright red embers swirled around them.

A shiver ran the length of Kirsty's spine. She felt a rush of wind coming straight up from the ground. Suddenly there didn't seem to be any air to breathe. In horror she saw the bushes in the crevice burst into flame. She reeled from the sudden onslaught of heat.

Jesse yanked at her arm, pulling her along the ledge so that the crevice was no longer beneath them. He cupped his hand around her ear.

"We have to get away from here! We have to jump! Now!"

He pushed off. Another swarm of burning embers fell around her, biting and burning. Dizzy with panic, Kirsty rolled over the side of the ledge.

She was in the air, dropping like a stone. Her feet hit solid rock. She couldn't find her balance, she was falling too quickly. Her head was going to hit the rocks. Then Jesse caught her shoulders and pulled her upright.

He grabbed her hand and yanked. Kirsty stumbled after him over slabs of slanting rock. He led the way into a hollow in the rock face. A slab of rock had split away, leaving a gap. Kirsty crawled in. Jesse was right behind her.

They huddled under a narrow ceiling of rock. Outside their shallow cave the fire raged. Kirsty looked at Jesse and saw he was just as terrified as she was.

She buried her face in her arms. A tiny bit of moisture leaked from her eyes, all her body could spare for tears. Jesse's hand found hers and held tight.

Save us. Please, let us live. Kirsty found herself praying, her lips forming soundless words that came from her heart. She could see the faces of her family as clearly as if they were right there in front of her: Mom; her dad and her stepmom,

Janice; her little brother, Brandon. And Lancelot, galloping down through the trees, his wide ears pricked as if he knew exactly where he was going.

The fire bellowed its fury. The rock walls trembled. There was no air. Kirsty felt herself falling down a long, dark tunnel, spinning and spinning. Colours and images blurred. Her strength was gone.

She let go and the terrible noise faded to silence.

9

"Kirsty! Wake up!" The voice was oddly hoarse; she couldn't recognize it.

"Come on, say something." She was so tired. She needed to rest, but now the person was shaking her by the shoulder. She opened her eyes and blinked, trying to see in the shadowy light. It was Jesse.

"Don't." That was her own voice, but it was also a barely recognizable croak.

"Where are we?" he demanded.

"I don't know. Jesse, leave me alone. I'm tired." She let her eyelids fall shut again.

He shook her once more. "Tell me where we are."

"Somewhere stinky. Yuck, someone's burning garbage." Her lungs burned. And then she remembered everything. "We're alive?"

"We are, Kirsty. We made it." He mumbled something under his breath. She thought he said "so far."

She heard his boots scuff against the rock. Squinting to see in the dimness, she watched him lean outside the cave.

"Come on, let's get out of here." His hand reached out and pulled her after him.

They were immersed in a fog of smoke. It was snowing, heavy white flakes of ash tumbling from the sky. She looked up at the top of the cliff. A dark haze curtained the rock face. She searched for the forest above the cliff, and for the trees and shrubs that had dotted the cliff face. There was nothing but drifting grey smoke.

Nothing. Everything was gone—trees, brush, leaves, every last cone and stick. Only blackened roots remained, tiny spot fires flickering as the flames fed on these last bones left over from the feast. Even the ground was smouldering, heavily carpeted in thick, black soot.

Below, the devastation vanished into the smoke.

"Jesse."

He turned, his head and shoulders dusted with white ash.

"You saved our lives," she said. She gestured to the smoking, barren landscape surrounding them. "If we'd been out there instead of in the cave…we couldn't have escaped."

"I didn't do it on purpose, Kirsty, you know that. I was just lucky to find it."

"You still saved our lives. You made me jump." She moved, and Lancelot's bit bumped against her ribs. She stared down at it in dismay. "Lancelot. Oh, no. No, no, no! Where are you? Where did you go? Lancelot!" she shrieked, choking on the smoke.

"Kirsty!" Jesse took her by the shoulders. "Listen to me. You have to stay calm."

"But Lancelot! He didn't want to leave me. What if—"

"Don't think that! He's a smart animal. He's got instincts humans have forgotten all about. He would've sensed the fire was coming and gotten away from here."

"But the fire came so fast, Jesse. How could he make it?"

He shrugged and shook his head. "Don't give up hope, Kirsty, not yet. Miracles do happen."

Above his ash-dusted bandana his dark eyes were serious. His fingers dug into her shoulders. "Don't give up on him."

Kirsty struggled to control her fear and panic. She nodded. "I won't."

"Good." He let go. "Come on, put on your bandana and let's get away from here."

They began negotiating the huge chunks of rock at the base of the cliff. There was no clear path for their feet to follow; every step had to be taken carefully between and around the rocks. Jesse stumbled and grabbed at a boulder to catch his balance. Instantly he snatched his hands away. "Ow! That's hot!" He blew on his palms. "Watch out, Kirsty, don't touch the rocks."

Kirsty nodded wearily. Her head pounded. Her nose, throat and eyes all burned from the smoke, and she was close to vomiting. Her mouth and tongue were dry and foul-tasting; every time she swallowed, the horrible flavour of smoke became stronger. Wood ash drifted through the air. Every inch of her was plastered in it—she could even feel it on her scalp.

The rock slabs broke up in a long, steep slide. She stopped and stood looking down at the slide, utterly exhausted. How was she possibly going to get over the rocks without breaking a leg or ankle? She watched dully as Jesse gingerly touched the rocks, testing for heat.

"It's okay, they're not so hot here." Then he began to crab-walk down the slide. "Come on, you can do it."

She folded to the ground. For a long time she didn't move, just sat there in misery. She couldn't go any farther, she just couldn't. Jesse was calling up to her. His voice was muffled by his bandana, but she didn't have to hear his words to know he was urging her on. She shook her head, refusing. No more. She could do no more. She shut her eyes and prayed for mercy, for rescue.

Jesse's hand grabbed her ankle and pulled. She bumped painfully down the rock slide.

Kirsty's mind drifted, leaving her struggling body behind. She let it wander far from this place, back to a time early in the summer when she and Faye had slept in the hayloft of the old barn at Hillcroft Farm, rising when the moon was still a pale shadow in the grey dawn sky. They'd danced on the damp grass in their pyjamas, laughing and giggling, gumboots on their bare feet—Faye had insisted. The ponies had watched them in fascination. The foals had joined in, whirling and leaping and cavorting, their fuzzy bottlebrush tails sticking straight up.

Even Lancelot had indulged in a playful buck or two, his thick tail swirling in the air. Her heart still warmed at the memory of him playing, fat and sassy, a far different pony than the thin, edgy animal she'd bought just months before.

"Keep moving," Jesse attempted to holler, voice cracking. "We're nearly there."

Kirsty jerked back to the present. Nearly where? She could hardly see past her hands and feet. The smoke obscured everything. She could hardly swallow for the fine ash coming in under her bandana and clogging her throat.

Jesse's arm snaked out of the smoke and caught her elbow. He towed her along, weaving in and out among the boulders littering the mountainside. He was moving too fast; her feet couldn't find the ground to keep up. She stumbled and he held her up.

"Slow down," she gasped.

He flung her arm over his shoulders, wrapped his arm around her waist and hoisted her along with him.

Like a three-legged race, Kirsty thought.

She shrank back as tall, dark forms loomed in the smoky shadows. Jesse tugged her along, and she realized they were back among trees. Tall, living trees with rough brown bark and brushy limbs. Twigs snapped as they pushed through brittle brush, their boots sliding on ash-slippery bunchgrass.

"Stop!" wheezed Kirsty. She pulled out of Jesse's grasp and bent over in a coughing fit. She stood up to see Jesse holding a finger in the air. He frowned.

"Do you feel that?"

A tendril of hair blew across her cheek. "The wind?"

He nodded. "It's changed direction. It's blowing the fire back. It's on our side now. Look."

Peering through the trees, Kirsty thought she could make out a faint light in the smoky darkness. She followed Jesse toward it. A stout breeze ruffled her hair. A few steps more and they moved into a translucent gold haze. She looked around. Trees, trees and more trees.

"Come on." Jesse started off.

Kirsty didn't move. "We're still lost."

Jesse looked back.

"When you're lost, you're supposed to stay in one place until someone finds you. I read that in a book." She dropped down cross-legged to the ground.

Jesse scowled at her. "Get up. Come on."

She shook her head.

"Don't be stubborn. You can't just stay here."

"I'm not following you anymore. You're getting us more and more lost. I'm staying right here until someone finds me."

Jesse crouched down beside her. "Listen, we don't even know if anyone's out looking for us yet. Even if they are, it could take hours, maybe even days, to find us. Meanwhile, there's a forest fire burning right on our tails. We can't just sit here, hoping to be rescued. We've got to save ourselves. Oh, come on, please don't cry."

"I'm not! I'm just so...tired."

"Me, too. We'll rest, for a little while. But we have to keep moving."

"I can't. I can't go any farther. I just can't. I wish I'd never come on this stupid cattle drive. I wish I was home, safe, with Lancelot."

Jesse patted her shoulder. "Wishing for the past doesn't do any good. Believe me, I know. We've got to deal with things the way they are. Truth is, Kirsty, there's no other choice."

10

The old white pony wouldn't load.

Patty propped her hands on her hips and frowned at the obstinate animal. "Listen, you, there isn't time for this kind of behaviour. Faye, get the lunge line."

Wearily, Faye dug a long line of thin nylon webbing out of a tack trunk in the front of the trailer. She didn't know how Patty managed to keep her steady calm. Faye was hot, tired, hungry and scared. They'd already hauled out one load of horses. After unloading them at the fairgrounds they had turned right around and come back without stopping for rest or food.

There was still no word of Lucy or Kirsty or the Hallidays.

She handed the long web line to Patty, who uncoiled it and passed one end behind the pony's tail to the farm's owner, Pete Mack, on the other side. "Okay, let's see if we can pull him on."

Together they heaved. The pony took a step toward the horse trailer, then balked. He teetered as his hind legs were pulled toward his front, but somehow he kept this stance without moving.

"You stubborn little so-and-so," scolded Pete as the pony sat down on his hind end like a big dog.

A truck roared into the yard. "Fifteen minutes! You've got fifteen minutes to get out of here!"

"I haven't got all my animals out," Pete protested.

"Turn them loose! The fire's heading for the road. You'll be cut off when it gets there. Get your family and leave right away!" The truck reversed and sped away.

"I'll get the old mare; she always loads." The owner shoved the pony's shank at Faye and hurried over to the corral.

Minutes later an elderly grey mare, four goats and a donkey were in the trailer. At the last moment the pony hopped on to join his companions. Patty slammed the doors shut behind him. "That's a full load."

"Thank goodness," said Pete. "My kids would never forgive me if we had to leave their pets behind."

"But what about those horses?" Faye pointed to a pair of black draft horses waiting patiently at a hitching rail.

"I'll have to turn them loose and hope they find their way out." Pete Mack strode over to the big horses and unclipped their lead ropes. He pulled off his cap and swatted their rumps. "Get out of here! Come on, get going!"

"Daddy! What are you doing to Nip and Tuck? Why are you hitting them?"

"Michael, come back here," shrieked his mother.

"Come on, we've got to go." Pete snatched up the little boy and hurried him into the waiting vehicle with the rest of his family. He folded into the driver's seat.

"No, no, don't leave Nip and Tuck!" the children screamed as the car drove off.

The blacks circled back and came to a stop in front of Faye. Ears flicking nervously, they regarded her with their dark brown eyes.

"Get in the truck, Faye," said Patty.

Faye opened the door. The horses followed her, their muzzles at her shoulder as she hopped up onto the seat. She pushed their heads away and slammed the door shut.

"They're not going anywhere," said Mr. Devries as Patty eased the truck and trailer along the bumpy driveway. "Let's hope they make it."

Faye pressed her face against the window. The blacks were still standing in the same place, watching the truck drive away.

"Those poor people. Can you imagine leaving your animals behind?" said Patty.

A picture flashed into Faye's mind: Sparrow, Blackbird, Grey Gull, Lancelot and all the other ponies staring with bewilderment after their trusted humans as they took off, abandoning them to their fates. She squirmed uneasily in her seat. Her feet tangled in something on the floor. She looked down and saw that the new lead ropes Patty had bought had slid out of their shopping bag.

It was a sign. Faye pulled the lead ropes onto her lap. She fumbled at the door latch. "Stop! Stop the truck!"

Patty stamped on the brake. "What's wrong?"

Faye needed her to put the vehicle in park to release the door locks. "The trailer doors—I think they're open," she lied.

"They can't be," said Patty. She shifted the truck's gears.

"I'll go check." Faye scrambled out of the truck and shut the door behind her.

"Faye? Is everything okay back there? Faye, what are you doing?"

Faye clipped a lead rope onto one of the big horses and guided him alongside the horse trailer. She slung the other rope over her shoulder and hopped up on the wheel well. "Steady, big fellow, just stand now." Muttering a quick prayer—she was never very good at getting on without a saddle—she bent her knees and sprang up, flinging herself at the horse.

She almost made it. She squirmed furiously, trying to pull herself onto the horse's back. His head came up high, and she prayed he wouldn't start moving, not now, not... there, she hooked her right elbow over the thick neck. She dug in, levering the rest of her body onto the wide chesterfield of a back. She bent her knee and dragged her leg over the animal's rump and onto the other side.

She was aboard. She gave a pat of thanks, then dug in her heels. Nip—or was it Tuck?—sprang forward. He whinnied, and his partner hurried into position on their right. Faye realized she wasn't going to need the second lead rope.

"Faye! What on earth!"

"Young lady, get back here right now!"

Hanging on to her mount's mane and lead rope with both hands, Faye risked a glance over her shoulder. Patty and Mr. Devries stood beside the truck, their faces wearing identical expressions of consternation.

"Don't worry, we'll be okay," she shouted, but the words were lost beneath the thundering bass drumbeat of the draft horses' trotting hooves.

"Jesse, do you really think Lancelot got away before the fire came? Or did he—" She couldn't finish her question. She couldn't let herself think of what might have happened to her pony. If she did, she'd begin to scream and never stop.

Jesse met her searching gaze. "*We* did, didn't we? And Lancelot's got better hearing, a better sense of smell, faster legs and a much better sense of direction."

"If only we knew which way he went, we could follow him. Jesse, do you think they're looking for us?"

"You mean the grandfolks and Lucy?" He nodded. "We're way overdue for meeting up with them. They would've figured out by now that something's gone wrong and come after us." He got to his feet. "Shh, I heard something."

"Do you see anything?"

He nodded. "There's something moving through the trees. Some kind of animal. Big. Really big."

Kirsty scrambled to her feet.

"Stay still, it's coming closer," hissed Jesse.

Tree boughs shimmied and dry brush crackled as the creature passed through the forest. It was travelling with a purpose, and it was coming straight for them.

Jesse snatched up a broken branch and held it before him like a sword. "If I tell you, run!"

"What about you?"

"I'll hold it off so you can get away." He brandished the branch.

"What if it's a bear or a cougar? All you've got is that stick."

"Shh!"

They both tensed as a steady thumping echoed through the trees. Jesse took up a warrior's stance.

The thudding grew louder. Patches of light and shadow darted between the trees. Holding her breath, listening hard, Kirsty was surprised the animal was making so much noise. There was something familiar about that marching beat.

Suddenly, Jesse pushed Kirsty behind him and charged, howling, into the forest. The shadow creature snorted and whirled away, melting into the dimness.

"Stop! Jesse, stop!" She ran after him and caught his arm. "It's Lancelot!" She darted past Jesse.

"What?" He lowered his stick. "Kirsty, are you crazy? Come back here!"

She spun around in the empty, smoke-darkened forest. "It was him. I know it was. I saw him."

"Look around, there's no pony. Hey, are you feeling okay? Smoke inhalation can cause confusion…"

"I'm not seeing things! It was Lancelot! And now you've scared him away. Lancelot! Come back!" She pursed her dried lips and tried to whistle.

"Look, calm down." Jesse tensed and brandished the stick again. "It's coming. What are you—Kirsty! Get back!"

"Lancelot, come here, pony."

"I don't believe this," Jesse said softly as Lancelot emerged from the trees.

The pony went up to Kirsty and laid his head over her shoulder. She wrapped her arms around his neck. "Believe it, Jesse. He found us."

Jesse dropped the stick and gently patted the pony's neck. "You crazy animal. Why didn't you get away when you could?"

"Because he's my friend," said Kirsty, "and that's what

friends do: look out for each other. Jesse, what's wrong?"

He turned away, hiding his expression. "Nothing. Just a bit sore."

"Where?"

"Look, drop it, will you. What are you—the police? Why does everything turn into a cross-examination with you? Can we get going?"

He fell into a sullen silence while Kirsty bridled Lancelot and checked the cinch. She got up into the pony's saddle, then pulled her boot from the stirrup.

A fierce scowl twisting his face, Jesse jammed his boot into the stirrup and swung aboard.

Kirsty and Jesse rode in silence for a long time.

"Sorry," Jesse growled finally.

Kirsty said nothing.

"I said: I'm sorry."

"I heard you. What for?"

"For treating you like that. It's not your fault."

"What do you mean?"

"Lancelot came back for you." He laughed bitterly. "He's a *pony*—an animal—but he came back."

"Jesse, what is it? What's bothering you so much that it makes you act like such a..."

"Jerk?" he supplied.

"You said so." Kirsty heard him heave a long sigh.

"What's the sense of talking about it? You won't listen, nobody does."

"I will. I promise you I will."

"It's a real mess. I don't know where to start."

"At the beginning. We've got lots of time."

There was a long pause. "Have you ever wanted something so bad it's all you can think about? Every moment, all day long, it's right there with you. And when you go to sleep you dream about it, all night long. Do you know what I'm talking about, Kirsty?"

"I do." It was exactly how she'd felt before Lancelot became hers. And lately a new dream had caught her imagination and filled her nightly slumbers. "I know just what you mean."

"Well, that's what hockey is for me—my whole life. I'm good at it, really good. Good enough to win a full scholarship to summer camp, all expenses paid."

"Oh, that's nice," said Kirsty, picturing a camp like the one she'd gone to for several summers with crafts and games and campfire singsongs. Camp had been fun, but she couldn't imagine how Jesse could prefer it to spending time at the ranch.

Then he explained: "You've got to understand, this wasn't just any camp. It was for top league players, the cream of the crop. The best of the best. It was my lucky break. I was on my way to the top. Then I did something stupid."

"What?"

"I took a car."

Kirsty gasped. "You stole a car!"

"No, we didn't steal it! We just...borrowed it."

"Jesse, you're not even old enough for a driver's licence! What were you thinking?"

"It seemed like a good idea at the time."

"How is taking a car, no, *stealing* a car ever a good idea?"

"Hey, it's not as bad as it sounds. We weren't going joyriding or anything. We just needed the car to get somewhere quick."

"Who's 'we'?"

"My friends and I. You see, my buddy Craig—his parents are really strict. They gave him a curfew just because he got a lousy grade in English. We were walking home one day after working out at the gym and stopped off for a cold drink. We met up with some other guys, and time got away on us. Suddenly it was nearly time for Craig to check in and we still had a long way to go to get to his house. Then this man drove up and went in the store and left his car running. Someone said we should drive Craig home. Everyone laughed like he was joking, but next thing I knew they were all in the car and Craig was pushing me into the driver's seat because I was the only one who'd ever driven before—Grandpa taught me on the tractor."

"Oh, Jesse." Kirsty shook her head.

"I didn't want to! I tried to get out, but Craig held the door shut."

"Then what happened?"

"The owner of the car came out of the store, and I... panicked. All the guys were yelling at me to get out of there, so I drove off. I didn't go far, just around the block, and pulled over. We were going to take off and leave the car there for the owner to find."

"And then?" Kirsty prompted.

"Well, the cops arrived."

"Oh, no! Did they arrest you?"

"They took us to the police station and called our parents."

"They must have been upset."

"Upset? They went ballistic. They wouldn't listen to anything I said. They gave me all kinds of punishments, but the worst was taking away my hockey scholarship. Then they dragged me off to counselling."

"What was that like?" Her mother was keen on counselling, but so far she hadn't managed to persuade Kirsty to go.

Jesse snorted. "A waste of time. I refused to go anymore, and then they threatened to keep me out of hockey altogether. I started skipping classes. Then, because I wouldn't stop 'acting out,' they shipped me out here for the summer. Now they've decided it'd be a good idea for me to be stuck out here for the whole school year."

"Well, what did you expect?" said Kirsty. "You stole a car! Of course they're going to punish you."

"Yeah, I know. I really messed up. It's just that—you know who got my scholarship?"

"Who?"

"Craig. My so-called best friend. See, he didn't get in the car. After, he denied having anything to do with taking the car. His parents were so proud of him for 'thinking for himself,' they didn't even get mad at him for breaking his curfew. Some people get all the luck."

Kirsty couldn't help thinking of her own situation. Every month she worried about putting in enough hours at Hillcroft Farm to pay for her pony's keep. She got good grades at school—her mom insisted on that—and sometimes she babysat on weekend evenings to make extra money.

Meanwhile, another girl she and Faye knew, Nicole Walsh, had everything handed to her—ponies, saddles, lessons. Anything she wanted, her parents bought for her, including Faye's star jumping pony, Robin. Every time Kirsty thought about Nicole she got a burning pain in her stomach. It was just so unfair that one person had so much without working for it at all.

Jesse seemed to be reading her mind. "You want to know what really sucks? Craig doesn't even need that scholar-ship—his parents are rich!"

"So that's why you've been so nasty to everyone."

"It's hard to be all upbeat and cheerful when your life has been ruined."

"Yes, but you don't have to take it out on everyone around you."

"I know, I know. I just can't seem to help myself. I'm sorry," he repeated. "I really am."

Kirsty could tell he was sincere. She twined her fingers through Lancelot's mane, mulling over what Jesse had told her. She thought back to how Lancelot had come into her life. She'd done everything she could, and many things she shouldn't have, so he could be hers.

"I tried to help a friend, and I ended up losing the biggest chance of my life," said Jesse. "Now everyone treats me like I'm some kind of criminal. It's not fair."

"You're right, Jesse, it's not. Hey, Lancelot, where are you going?"

The pony had abruptly changed course, travelling across the side of the mountain instead of downhill. Kirsty corrected him, but he ignored the reins, shaking his head against the bit.

"Turn him back," Jesse said as the pony suddenly hiked up the steep slope.

"He won't listen! Lancelot!"

The pony heaved up and onto flat ground. Kirsty slacked off the reins.

"It's a road."

They looked in awe at the overgrown dirt road.

"Which way?" Jesse asked.

They were on level ground. In both directions the road faded into a swirling smoky haze. Lancelot held still, his head high and his ears flicking back and forth as he scented the air. Abruptly he moved off.

"How do you know this is the right way?" asked Jesse.

"I don't," confessed Kirsty. "I didn't choose. He did."

"Let him go. Give him his head."

Kirsty wrapped the reins around the saddle horn. "Okay, Lancelot, take us home."

The road suddenly climbed up.

"I don't like this," said Kirsty. Her fingers twitched, aching to grab the reins and turn the pony around and head the other way, which surely went downhill.

"Be patient. Give him a chance," urged Jesse.

A bend emerged in the smoke. Lancelot shifted his weight back onto his haunches. They came out of the turn onto a downward slope. The pony picked up his pace.

"He knows where he's going," said Jesse. "Lancelot, we should have listened to you a long time ago."

11

Faye hadn't gone far down the road when the truck and rattling horse trailer pulled alongside. The draft horses didn't even flinch. Patty leaned out the open window.

"Please, Faye, get in the truck now. Those horses will be fine."

"Don't worry about me. I'll be—"

"*Of course* we're worried about you!" roared Mr. Devries. "Get off that horse right now!"

He hardly ever raised his voice. Faye steeled her nerve. "I'm sorry, sir, but I can't do that."

"Faye, what about your grandmother? She trusts us to look after you. What are we supposed to tell her?" asked Patty.

"Tell her the truth, that I'm bringing out two horses that needed to be rescued. I'll explain everything. Don't worry, I'll make sure she doesn't blame you."

Patty shook her head. "Faye, we're not worried about getting blamed. We're worried about your *safety*. This is an evacuated area; we can't just go off and leave you behind.

You need to come with us."

"I can't. What if they were our horses—you'd want someone to save them, wouldn't you?"

"But they aren't our horses! They aren't even valuable!" said Mr. Devries. "They're just…horses! They aren't worth risking your life for!"

"I think they are."

"You are being very stubborn."

"I'm sorry, but I can't just leave them behind. I have to help them. It's…it's the right thing to do."

"Well, there's no time to argue. We're coming back for you right away. Just keep those big horses moving as fast as they can go," said Patty. "And Faye, stay *safe*. That's an order, get it?"

She nodded. "I get it."

"No, Patty, this is foolishness. We can't leave her behind!" Mr. Devries was still protesting as Patty drove off.

"We'll be okay. Right, boys?" She patted the sturdy black neck in front of her.

Except for the clomping of the big horses' feet, it was quiet. Unnaturally quiet. No birds, no insects, nothing.

It was impossible to see where they were. They were immersed in a haze of smoke. It was everywhere, above, below, all around. Faye felt it scratching her eyes, burning her nose and throat. She tugged her T-shirt collar over her nose as a filter.

The big blacks had nothing. She imagined the smoke rushing into those wide, round nostrils and down the windpipe into their lungs. "We'll get you looked after. Just as soon as we reach safety, you'll be taken care of. I'll make sure of it."

The broad ears were turned back, listening to her voice. Abruptly, they snapped forward. Both big heads rose up high. She felt her mount's steps slow. He whinnied, his partner doing the same a half beat behind him.

Through the smoke ahead a long chorus of whinnies echoed back to them.

"Look, I owe you big time," said Jesse. "Is there anything you need? Anything you want? You might have to wait until I'm rich and famous, but I won't forget, I promise you."

Kirsty shook her head. "Jesse, we're even. I helped you and you helped me."

"And Lancelot helped us both. What does he want—a ton of carrots?"

"Sure, Jesse, Lancelot loves carrots. But a bag would be plenty."

"What about you? There must be something you want."

Kirsty pondered the question. For so long, all she'd wanted was a pony. Now she had Lancelot and, along with him, a whole new life complete with friends and adventures. She couldn't imagine wanting anything more.

Except…not so very long ago, just a few weeks back, she'd had a dream. It had stayed with her when she woke. She'd kept it close and secret, playing it in her head while she filled water troughs and picked out corrals and brushed through manes and tails. It was bright and exciting and as fragile as glass. As long as she didn't tell anyone, it would stay like that, safe from ridicule and mockery.

And that's all it would ever be—a dream. But wasn't that what they were talking about, dreams coming true?

"I want a pony sanctuary," she blurted. "A place where unwanted and neglected ponies can live and be cared for. Some of them—the ones that are young and sound—could get training. That's the problem with so many unwanted animals: they haven't ever been properly trained. And then, once they're fixed up, they could go to new owners. There could be a training course for the owners to learn how to handle ponies properly—Lucy could help me set that up."

"Wow. You've put a lot of thought into this," said Jesse.

"It just came into my head a little while ago. I was riding Lancelot one day at the farm, and Lucy had some people over looking for a pony to buy. They asked me if Lancelot was for sale. Of course I said no, but that got me thinking. Just months ago nobody wanted this pony because he was so badly behaved. All it took was some time and train- ing, and now he's so good people want to buy him. We were lucky; we've had Lucy and Faye teaching us. I don't know what would have happened without their help. But I started wondering about all the other unwanted ponies out there and how to help them." She took a deep breath. "And that's it. That's what I want."

Jesse said nothing.

She should have kept her mouth shut, Kirsty realized. This was what always happened when she opened up and let her heart out. No one understood.

"Kirsty, that is the most—"

"Crazy idea you've ever heard," she finished for him. "Look, forget I said anything, please. It's just a dream; it'll never happen. Where would the money come from? I can barely get enough to look after one pony."

"Where would the money come from?" echoed Jesse. "That *is* the big question. Hmm. I'll have to think on that one."

He was making fun of her. "Just drop it, okay?"

"Kirsty, listen—"

"Please. I don't want to talk about it anymore. Forget I said anything."

He settled his hands on her shoulders, squeezing lightly. "Don't be upset. Hey! The smoke's clearing off."

It was true. The grey haze was drifting apart, revealing ranks of trees all around them. Kirsty tugged down her bandana to breathe in soft, sweet air. She peered through the trees.

"Do you see that? Up ahead."

Jesse leaned over her shoulder. His fingers dug in. "It's got to be. It just has to."

A pale light broke through the dark blue background of trees, directly in front of them. Lancelot hurried toward it. The light became bright and wider.

The trees parted. Kirsty caught glimpses of golden fields, the bright green of an irrigated alfalfa field, the faded red of an old barn.

The dirt road bent down in a final, steep descent. Lancelot's hooves rang out on asphalt. They were on level ground, travelling on the edge of a paved road running along a meadow. On the far side the grassy field dropped away, a row of treetops marking its descent. Off in the distance, a heavily treed mountain rose steeply.

"We made it! We're back on the flats," Jesse cheered. "Kirsty, we got out!"

She gazed around her in wonderment. After so many hours of seeing nothing but trees and rocks, the empty pastures and silent buildings seemed unreal, like a movie set.

"We made it," she whispered, trying to convince herself. They were lost no longer. They had found their way back.

So why didn't it feel safe?

"Where is everyone?" she asked.

"I don't know. Look." Jesse pointed at a pink plastic ribbon fluttering on a fence post at the end of a driveway.

"There's another. And another. Jesse, every place has one. There are pink ribbons all the way along the road."

"What do they mean? And where are we? I don't recognize any of these houses...wait, yes, I do! There's Larry's cabin, over there in those trees."

"How far are we from the ranch?"

"A long way. But at least we know we're going in the right direction. Hey, easy now!"

Kirsty grabbed for the saddle horn as Lancelot suddenly scooted across the pavement. Hastily she unwound the reins from the saddle horn and pulled him to a halt. A car roared up beside them. The driver stuck his head out the window. He shouted to be heard over the children crying in the back seat.

"What are you kids doing? This area's been evacuated. The fire's coming this way. Come on, get in."

"Go ahead, Kirsty."

"No, you go. You're hurt."

"Both of you—get in the car!"

"I'm not leaving my pony."

"And I'm not leaving *her*."

The driver slapped the steering wheel. "Look, this isn't a joke. There's a fire right on our tails. We've got to get out of here!"

A woman leaned across the front seat. "Please, come with us. We'll get you to safety."

"Thank you, but—"

"You kids are crazy. Just crazy!" The driver shifted the car into gear.

"Pete, we can't just leave them!"

"We can't waste any more time. One last chance—are you coming?"

Kirsty shook her head.

"Listen, you get that pony moving as fast as he can." Pete studied them hard, memorizing their faces. "We'll be praying for you."

The car sped off. Moments later it went over a rise in the road and disappeared.

"Hang on!" Kirsty dug her boot heels into Lancelot. Ahead, over the clopping of his trotting hooves, they heard a car horn blaring.

Lancelot's head rose high. His rib cage pushed out as he whinnied, over and over.

Suddenly, a carillon of hoofbeats rang out on the pavement. A herd of horses filled the road before them, galloping full out. Eyes white-ringed with fear, nostrils distended, necks and flanks stained with sweat, they charged unchecked at the pony with his double riders.

Kirsty held hard on the reins as the herd swarmed around them and Lancelot plunged and reared, wildly excited. Jesse cried out as he tumbled to the pavement. Kirsty leaned over to look for him among the prancing hooves.

Lancelot bucked, shaking her boots out of the stirrups. He bucked again, and the saddle horn punched her in the ribs. Once more and she was sliding down the stirrup fender.

Jesse grunted as she landed on him. She staggered to her feet.

"Whoa! Lancelot, whoa! Come back!"

"Save your breath, he's gone," huffed Jesse, slowly pushing himself upright. "You okay?"

"I think so. How about you?"

"Hurting." He groaned. "That must mean I'm still alive."

Side by side they watched the herd of horses, Lancelot among them, gallop off into the distance.

"Lancelot! Come back," shrieked Kirsty.

"Kirsty, he's following his herd instinct—he's not going to listen to you."

"Where did all those horses come from?"

"I'm guessing they've been turned loose to escape the fire. That means it's getting close. Come on, we've got to get out of here." Jesse started to walk down the centre of the pavement. He looked back over his shoulder. "Where are you going?"

"I have to get Lancelot."

"He's with all those horses; he'll be all right."

"But they're going the wrong way. Don't they know they're heading toward the fire?"

"They're panicking, Kirsty. They're probably going back home, the last place they felt safe."

"So what are we going to do—just leave them behind to get burned alive?"

"You heard that man: this road's been evacuated. We can't go back."

"Lancelot's my friend. He saved our lives. If it wasn't for him, we'd still be lost up on the mountain. I can't just leave him behind. I have to try to get him out."

Jesse turned around.

"You don't have to come," she told him.

"That's what you think. I can imagine what Grandpa Stuart would have to say if I showed up without you. I'll take my chances on being burned alive." He grabbed her hand and began to jog down the road, towing Kirsty beside him.

Within a few minutes she was tugging his hand to slow down. "I can't breathe."

Jesse halted. "Me neither. It's like there's no oxygen in the air."

Kirsty could taste ash again as she dragged in mouthfuls of air. Heat pressed down on her neck and shoulders, a heavy wool blanket she couldn't shake off.

Her breathing steadied. "It's so quiet," she said.

"I know. It's…creepy." Jesse tensed.

Kirsty followed his gaze. Like gathering storm clouds, white smoke puffed over the crest of the mountains, massing across the sky.

Ahead, a horse whinnied.

"That sounds close." Jesse pulled her along.

Around a bend they saw the herd swerve into a driveway. Jesse ducked through a rail fence, cutting across a field. "Close the gates," he shouted when Kirsty caught up.

She swung a tall pole gate across the entrance to the farm. It met up with Jesse's gate in the middle of the driveway. They wrestled the latch shut and turned around. The herd had fragmented, horses dashing frantically around the farmhouse and outbuildings.

"Lancelot!" Kirsty chased her pony down on the front lawn, cornering him against a stand of lilacs. "Whoa, pony, whoa! Easy now, it's me."

Sides heaving, the pinto dropped his head and moved toward her. Kirsty snagged his reins. He'd stepped on one, breaking it off short.

Jesse was pulling a bicycle out of a shed when she led Lancelot around the house. "Check in the barn for some baler twine. You can use it for a rein."

"Why don't you just ride one of the horses? There must be a bridle in the barn."

"Except for a couple of mares with foals, they're all young stock. Who knows if they're broke yet. At least this bike isn't going to buck me off. Hurry up and fix that rein so you can help me round up these horses."

"What for?"

"Well, we aren't going to leave them behind, are we?"

The barn was a single-storied, modern building with a wide alley down the middle and sliding doors at each end. Leading Lancelot inside, Kirsty was surprised to see every one of the stalls had a horse inside, even though the stall doors were wide open. Playing out the unbroken rein to the very end, she went into the feed room and found an old feed sack stuffed with discarded bale twine. She pulled out three lengths, Lancelot jerking at the end of the rein.

"Be patient," she scolded him.

He rattled a bucket hooked over a standpipe beside the alley. Water! Kirsty couldn't believe she hadn't thought of it. She filled the bucket with water. While the pony drank, she hastily braided the twine and tied it to the bit. Lancelot lifted his head and sighed, water dribbling from his lips.

"My turn." Kirsty cranked open the spout and let water splash into her mouth and over her face and neck, sluicing away the sweat and grime, soothing parched tissues. The relief was enormous. She bent her head and let the water run down the back of her neck into her scalp.

"What's taking you so long? Oh, water!"

Kirsty moved back to let Jesse have a drink. As he soaked his head, she tried to coax a horse out of its stall.

"Out you come, you can't stay in there. Come on, don't be so stubborn."

"This must be their own barn," said Jesse, looping his belt over the horse's neck. He led it out. "They think they'll be safe in their stalls."

Lancelot jumped back as Kirsty swung the stall door shut. A flip of his head and the reins were pulled out of her hand. Ears pricked, he ducked out the back of the barn, whinnying.

"Can't you hang on to that animal?" Jesse said, exasperated.

"I'll be right back." Kirsty ran after the pony.

Lancelot trotted past a corral and around the side of a long, low-roofed shed.

"Whoa! Now stand still." Kirsty caught up the reins again. "Why did you—oh, no! Jesse! Jesse, come quick! Hurry!"

"What? What is it?" He took in the scene inside the shed. "Oh...crap."

A palomino mare dashed back and forth along the open side of the long shed. Inside the rundown building a golden-haired foal had broken through the plywood floor. Both front legs had punched hoof-sized holes in the rotten wood. The hind legs were sunk up to the hocks. Startled by Kirsty and Jesse's sudden appearance, the foal renewed its struggle, frantically attempting to move all four limbs. The plywood splintered with a loud crack, and the foal's hind end slipped further into the hole.

The mare neighed hysterically, nearly colliding with Lancelot in her panic. Her long white tail lashed against her corn-yellow flanks, and she stomped her front feet menacingly.

"Whoa, whoa there! Steady now, easy, little one." Jesse was on his knees, crawling over the plywood to the foal's head. He caught the halter and stroked the animal's neck, his hand leaving streaks in the sweat. The foal's eyes were white-ringed with fear, its nostrils distended and pink centred.

"Jesse, be careful," Kirsty called.

"That's it, settle down now," Jesse crooned to the foal, all the while stroking its head and neck. Gradually, the rolling eyes became still and the little ears turned toward him. The foal ceased fighting and hung quivering in its wooden trap. "It's going to be okay. We'll get you out."

"We have to get help. We can't do this on our own," said Kirsty.

"There isn't time." Jesse rocked back on his heels, rubbing at his chin.

"Jesse! Look how big it is. We'll never lift that foal out by ourselves."

It was true. Close to weaning, the foal was already bigger than the smallest of Lucy's ponies, and stout.

Jesse slowly crawled away and stood up. "Kirsty, you look around for some bales of hay or straw, at least four, more would be better. Bring them here. I've got to get some tools."

The hay was stored in a huge stack under a pole building behind the barn. Lancelot dove at it, ripping at the stalks hungrily. Kirsty slipped his bit out of his mouth and left him to eat. She found a wheelbarrow and stacked it high. Picking up the handles to push the wheelbarrow, she glanced up at the mountains towering over the farm and froze. The mountaintops were rimmed with fire. She threw her weight against the wheelbarrow and rushed it to the shed.

"Jesse, hurry, the fire's right above us!"

He grunted and kept on sawing a hole at the edge of the plywood. The foal was quiet, sunk in dull-eyed misery. Its mother stood close by, giving gentle, encouraging nudges with her soft muzzle. Her dark eyes regarded Jesse warily.

"Where do you want this hay?"

"Stack it right beside me."

When she returned with the second load, Jesse had cut a hole the size of a hay bale in the wood floor. He stomped one foot on the cut-out and it broke away. Kirsty heard a hollow thump as it landed.

"There's nothing under that floor!"

Jesse nodded. "It's a grease pit. It's all dug out underneath. You pull away the plywood and park your tractor over this hole. Then you climb down into the pit and change the oil or whatever. This plywood's rotten. It should have been replaced a long time ago."

He grabbed a hay bale and stuffed it down through the cut-out into the pit. More bales followed. Crouching on his hands and knees, he peered into the pit.

"Look out!"

He rolled away as the foal began to thrash about. The mare nickered and pawed anxiously. "Go to its head, Kirsty. Talk to it, get it to stay still."

Kirsty squatted at the foal's head, rubbing her hand up and down the long white blaze. The mama horse was still pawing, her knee bumping Kirsty's leg. "Jesse, what are you doing? Are you crazy? Get out of there, you'll get kicked!"

"Stay calm and don't upset that foal, not right now." Jesse had lowered himself into the pit. "Be right back. I hope." He ducked out of sight.

Kirsty forced her voice low and soothing. "Easy, little fellow, that's a good boy. Or girl. Easy now, nice and quiet, that's the way. Steady." She drew out the word into a long sigh.

The foal's ears twitched. Its eyes rolled back, and the muscles in its hind end bunched.

"Jesse, watch out!"

The foal erupted. Splinters of wood scattered as it

surged up out of the hole, legs flailing wildly. One front hoof wrenched free of the plywood and then the other. Bent kneed, the foal heaved out of the hole onto the packed dirt of the shed. Kirsty shrank back against the wall as it scrambled on stiff legs to its mother's side. Both horses rushed out of the building.

"Jesse!" She dropped beside the cut-out. She could see his body curled up in a corner. "Oh, no, Jesse." She swapped ends, hanging her feet into the hole.

"Don't come down. There isn't much room."

"Are you all right?"

"I think so." His head popped out. "That was close."

"You idiot! You could have been killed. Why did you go down there?"

"I had to get the hay bales under the foal's feet so she'd have something to push against. Oh, she's a filly, by the way."

Kirsty rocked back on her heels. "That was a really brave thing to do."

Jesse shrugged. "It worked." He reached for her to help him out of the pit, wincing, Kirsty knew, at the pain in his ribs. "How's the foal? Is she hurt at all?"

"I didn't notice," Kirsty admitted. "She got right out of here quick. But she seemed to be moving okay."

"We'd better get out of here quick, too."

"Jesse, do you think the herd came back for the mare and her foal?"

He shrugged. "Maybe. Horses are herd animals; they stick together. But it was Lancelot who took us right to them. He's the hero."

Outside the shed, Kirsty noticed that smoke was thickening the air. Automatically, her eyes went to the mountain. A heavy blanket of smoke covered the steep slopes. All she could see of the fire was glowing bursts of amber and scarlet beneath the dense charcoal-grey wool.

The palomino mare was nursing her filly near the corral when Kirsty returned, leading Lancelot. Free of her prison the filly was much calmer, breaking off nursing to give them a sniffing as they checked her limbs.

"That's amazing," said Jesse. "She's pretty scuffed up and that hock is swollen, but nothing looks too bad." He cradled the filly's head in his hands and rubbed his nose against her velvet muzzle.

A gust of wind rattled the metal roof of the shed behind them.

"Let's get out of here."

Jesse ran to open the gates while Kirsty, on Lancelot, gathered the horses and pushed them back down the driveway onto the main road. The wind sputtered, tossing about a drifting haze of smoke. The light had changed, taking on a muted amber hue.

Behind the silvery smoke curtain, the entire horizon was aglow.

Kirsty pulled up Lancelot to stare. From mountainside to mountainside, across the wide flats of the ridge and into the sky overhead, rippled a wall of shimmering gold. She couldn't tear her eyes away: it was the most beautiful, terrifying sight she'd ever seen.

Lancelot suddenly lifted his head, his body at rigid attention. He blew hard through his nostrils, a sharp blast of warning.

Kirsty settled her free hand over the horn.

"What is it?" called Jesse, catching up on the bike.

"I don't know. Something's spooking him...listen!"

Kirsty held her breath. There it was: a steady thumping, nearly a perfect rhythm. She wasn't imagining it; the pavement was shaking very slightly.

She glanced at the herd. Heads were high, ears at attention. The foals crowded close to their mothers' flanks.

The thumping was clearly audible now. She let out her breath.

"Can you see anything?" asked Jesse softly.

She squinted into the haze. "I'm not sure...yes, I can. It's big, really big. Look!"

Through the swirling grey smoke emerged two giant black war horses prancing up the road at them, necks curved, snorting and tossing their rippled manes.

Kirsty and Jesse gaped at the immense medieval creatures before them, characters in a fairy tale come to life.

Except that high on the broad back of one big horse was not a knight in shining armour but a single bareback rider.

Kirsty squinted again. Was the smoke playing tricks on her eyes? That hair, shining like a flame. It could only be…"*Faye?*"

"Hello? Hello? Is someone there? Please, help me. Help me get out of here."

12

"You can't go that way." Faye flung her arm out behind her. "The road's blocked—the power line came down. There's no way around it. The fire's coming, we've got to get away!"

Kirsty urged Lancelot up to the big horses. "Faye, what are you doing here? Where did you get those horses?"

"Kirsty? Is that really you? Oh my goodness, we've been so worried; nobody knew where you were. Where's my grandma?"

"We don't know."

"What do you mean? Did something happen to her? Tell me!"

"Jesse and I, we've been lost for hours."

"Jesse? Jesse Sims?"

"Right here. Come on, there's no time for all this talking. We've got to get going."

The wind stirred, tossing up grit into their faces.

"But the road—we can't get through!" cried Faye.

"We'll go across the fields," said Jesse.

"How?" asked Kirsty, looking quickly around at the taut barbed-wire boundary fences.

"We'll need wire cutters. We have to go back through the farm."

Just as they got the horses moving back into the farm driveway, a shower of sparks glittered through the air. They tumbled into the long, paper-dry grass along the fences, crackling into a myriad of tiny fires.

The lead horses whirled around, pushing the followers back in their fright.

"Block that end," called Kirsty. Faye moved the big horses across the driveway.

"It's no good," said Jesse. "They won't go past the fires!"

"We'll show them how. Come on, Lancelot."

Lancelot balked, his body rigid with fear. "Get up, Ponyboy, please. It's okay, you can do this." Kirsty clucked and chirped and drummed her heels, urging the pony forward. He stretched out his neck, snorting suspiciously at the fires snapping on both sides of the narrow road. "Please, Lancelot, go!"

He bounded ahead, galloping past the fires. On the other side he swung around and whinnied to the other horses.

"Good boy. Thank you."

Eyes rolling, the herd swept down the driveway after him. Burning embers twirled in the wind, pinging down on metal roofs. Jesse dropped the bike and flung open a pasture gate. He ran into the tool shed.

The herd swarmed into the pasture and galloped to the farthest end.

"Hurry, Jesse!"

He sprinted from the shed, stuffing a pair of fencing pliers in his back pocket. Faye shrugged the second lead rope from her shoulder and clipped it to Tuck.

"Here, get on!" While Faye struggled to hold the big horses still, Kirsty dismounted and boosted Jesse up onto the spare. "Let's go!"

Lancelot tore the reins through her grip. "Wait, I'm not on!" She ran beside him, clinging to the horn.

The big blacks were pulling away. It was now or never. Kicking her right leg high, Kirsty vaulted up into the saddle.

She didn't make it. Her leg had hooked over the broad seat, but she began to slide back down. She braced her arms and dug her fingers into the horn, trying to pull herself up, but she kept slipping.

Her thigh muscles strained. Her right knee had hooked against the high seat back, holding her steady.

Summoning all her strength, Kirsty squirmed up and onto the seat. She was aboard.

She dug her boots into Lancelot and flapped the reins. "Go! Go, go, go!"

Stirrups slapping empty, the pony galloped headlong down the sloping field to join the herd.

Coming over a rise, the riders saw a long line of rail fencing blocking access to the fields beyond.

"This way," said Jesse, swinging his mount to the left. He kicked the big horse into a trot, his head turned to watch some point in the distance.

Kirsty followed his gaze. She squinted, wondering if she was imagining the puddle of green sprawled along the horizon. For a brief moment, she thought she saw a glint of red beneath the green. Then a silvery haze wafted down from the smoke-wreathed mountain above, drawing over the scene like a net curtain.

"Come on!" Jesse galloped off, following the fenceline.

Lancelot sprinted after him. Soon the fastest horses in the herd were overtaking them, clouds of dust puffing up from their hooves. Kirsty looked back. There was Faye, clinging grimly to her horse's mane as he charged along in pursuit of his partner.

A cross fence was coming up on them. Jesse pulled up his horse, tossing the lead rope to Kirsty as she came alongside. He slid down and threw open a gate.

Somewhere off in the distance, a horse whinnied.

Lancelot flung up his head, his ears at alert. He screamed a reply, over and over and over.

Jesse climbed onto his horse from the fence. His eyes met Kirsty's, and he nodded. "We made it."

Faye rode up beside them. "That whinny—it sounds like Blackbird."

Jesse checked over his shoulder. "Looks like the herd's all through the gate. Come on, let's go!"

When they rode into the ranch yard, the gate to the largest corral was wide open. Stuart stood well back so the horses wouldn't be startled. He rested his chin in his hand, his eyes shaded beneath the low brim of his hat. Further along, Lucy and Midge sat atop the fence dividing the house from the outbuildings, Blackbird grazing behind them.

The herd milled about the ranch yard, raising dust. A couple of horses spun around, spooked by the strange surroundings. Kirsty raced after them, Lancelot's legs churning. He cut into the breakaways' path, turning them back into the herd. With the big blacks pushing up from behind, Kirsty and Lancelot chivvied and harried the horses into the corral. As the last rump passed through the gate, Stuart hurried over and swung it shut.

Jesse vaulted down. "Grandma! Grandpa! You're all right?"

"We're fine, son," said Stuart. He swallowed hard to clear his throat. "Just fine."

"Whew, that's a relief. We were worried about you."

"Well, I can understand that. We were worried sick about you kids. We tried to find you, but the fire turned us back..." His voice choked.

"I'm sorry. We got lost." Jesse squared his shoulders. "It was my fault. Totally. We would have been back sooner except we came across these horses. I didn't think we should leave them behind, not with the fire so close."

"Jesse, come here." Stuart reached for his grandson and hugged him. "I am so proud of you."

"So am I," said Midge, joining the embrace.

"Hi, Grandma!" Faye slid to the ground, grinning impishly. "Surprised to see me?"

"You bet I am. You've got some explaining to do, young lady," Lucy mumbled into her granddaughter's curls as she held her tight.

Kirsty took Lancelot up to the water trough. As the pony drank, she slacked off the saddle cinch. A hand settled on her shoulder. She looked into Lucy's sharp green eyes, full of concern and relief all at once.

"You okay?"

Kirsty's belly rumbled. She grinned ruefully. "I'm kind of hungry, and very thirsty. Otherwise, I'm good now that we're here at the ranch."

"I watched you turn back those horses. That was some impressive riding. You've got it now, girl. You're not a greenhorn, not anymore."

"Thanks, Lucy. That means a lot to me."

"It's nothing but the truth. Listen, Kirsty, I'm sorry. About what you went through today. It must have been terrifying. I should never have brought you along."

Kirsty's eyes filled with tears. "It was really scary, but..." She searched for the words to explain. "I found out things, Lucy, just like you said would happen. About what I'm made of. I can do a lot more than I thought I could. So please, don't be sorry, because the truth is I'm glad I came."

Then her newfound courage urged her to fling her arms around Lucy's wiry frame and hug the old woman tightly.

"You hold a special place in my heart," Lucy whispered, resting her cheek on top of Kirsty's hair. "You're my second granddaughter."

And Kirsty felt her heart stretching as it filled with love.

13

"Look at her go! Wow, that girl can ride," said Jesse admiringly as Faye urged Elan for more speed, galloping across the grass to leap a huge wall, then twisting around, the black mare nearly flat on her side, and racing to a double combination.

"Steady, Faye," cautioned Kirsty.

Over the oxer, then two strides, Elan rocking back onto her hocks to clear the second jump.

Jesse's hand grabbed Kirsty's. "One more."

"She's going too fast; she missed the inside turn."

"Doesn't matter, she's nearly two seconds ahead. She did it! She's clear!"—as Elan exploded over the final fence. Jesse flung his arms around Kirsty, lifting her off the ground in a bear hug.

"She won! She won!" Startled, Lancelot shot to the end of his lead shank, jerking Kirsty after him. She reeled him in, comforting him with a gentle pat and soft words.

"Are you ready?" Jesse tugged a clean rag from his back pocket and wiped it over Lancelot's already gleaming checkerboard coat. He smoothed the pony's mane, unusually silky and soft after the application of mane-and-tail shampoo and conditioner donated by the manufacturer. He dusted his own shoes with the rub rag, then shrugged on a sports coat over his periwinkle-blue shirt and straightened his tie. "Hey, what's wrong?"

"I can't do this. I can't go out in front of all those people." Kirsty pushed the stiff new leather lead shank at him.

"Whoa, whoa, steady now. Kirsty, what's the matter?"

"I feel sick. My stomach, I might throw up." She tried to swallow away the bile rising in her throat.

The loudspeaker blared, announcing the results of the junior grand prix for the Fire Victims' Benefit Horse Show. Faye was in first place on Elan, fourth with Ebon.

"I'll get you some water."

"No, don't go. Jesse, you'll have to take him in."

Jesse's dark eyes narrowed. He glared down at her, reminding Kirsty of the sullen boy she'd first met. "You're chickening out."

"Uh-huh," she agreed. Her teeth were chattering.

Faye and Elan entered the ring at the head of a parade of eight horses. She rode over to the presentation area and vaulted down, handing the mare's reins to a beaming Laurence Devries.

"Kirsty, this isn't about you," Jesse said sternly. "Or me. It's about Lancelot. Do it for him."

She closed her eyes and took a deep breath. "You're right. This is Lancelot's day."

A woman with a headset beckoned them over to the gate. "They're right here," she said into the mouthpiece.

Sparks of light flashed off the silver trophy Faye held over her head. Waves of cheering rolled out of the stands.

"How many people are here today?" Kirsty wondered.

"Ten thousand, maybe more," said the headset woman. "We get three times that at the fall tournament."

"Ten…thousand?" Kirsty squeaked.

The woman looked at her reassuringly. "Don't be nervous. Just imagine them all sitting there in their underwear."

Kirsty grimaced. "Oh, that doesn't help."

Then Jesse began to laugh, his eyes twinkling again. Kirsty's mouth twitched into a grin.

Lancelot screamed a greeting as Elan flew past, leading the victory gallop around the huge grass ring. Patty lurched by on a wildly excited Ebon, bucking and kicking out in time to the waltz music blasting over the public address system.

"Okay, you're on. Just go across to the presentation table."

The gate was opened. Lancelot plunged through it, towing Kirsty beside him. Jesse ran to catch up on the pony's far side.

"And now, ladies and gentlemen, we come to a very

special part of our program today: the Quality Mills Feed Special Hero Award."

Lancelot froze, his head high. As still as a statue, he surveyed the crowd of thousands around them, all staring in his direction. Then, bowing his neck, his thick tail arched high, he marched across the endless carpet of clipped green grass with immense dignity.

Kirsty raised her head high. She forgot her nerves, forgot to be intimidated by the huge crowd, forgot her discomfort at wearing a dress and shoes with heels instead of her usual jeans and boots. Her heart swelled with pride at the gleaming, prancing creature that was Lancelot transformed. Her pony, her friend, her saviour.

Television cameras filmed their procession as the announcer told their story, two lost people rescued and carried to safety through a raging forest fire by a brave, stalwart pony. Kirsty blinked at the sudden prickling in her eyes.

She was delighted Lancelot was getting the honour and recognition he deserved, and yet there were so many others whose courage and selfless generosity had gone unnoticed.

Or had it? She remembered the joyful tears of the young couple when they discovered their small herd of horses, including a three-month-old palomino filly, was safe and sound in the riverside pastures of Mountainridge Ranch.

The children hugging the legs of a pair of patient black

draft horses. The stern-featured old man, crossing and uncrossing his arms when reunited with his tiny flock of rare wool sheep, finally raising his eyes skyward and muttering a few words before kneeling to hug the pair of guardian dogs that had never deserted their charges.

For many long days the inferno had challenged the fire-guards. The exhausted firefighters never faltered, standing their ground until the fire changed course, pushed by the winds to retreat deep back into the mountains to consume hectares and hectares of forest. A smoke-pearled haze and orange horizon held in the skyline for weeks until the long-prayed-for rains came, soothing the earth like a balm and rinsing the sky clear again.

Wildlife had perished. So had cattle, caught out on the range. A man had been rushed to hospital during the evacuation and died there of a heart attack, believed to have been brought on by stress and fear.

Three houses and numerous outbuildings had burned down. Only three homes—a miracle, people told each other. For the three families left homeless, a disaster.

The community had come together, feeding and housing and comforting each other. A time of sorrow and gratitude tangled together.

"Kirsty."

Jesse's voice broke into her memories. They were at the presentation area, and the announcer turned to the audience to introduce a small crowd of dignitaries. She was surprised to see Laurence Devries standing among them.

Beneath the announcer's amplified voice, she heard her name being called. Squinting into the stands, she saw her mother waving furiously. Beside her were Kirsty's stepmother, Janice, and Dad and Brandon. She lifted her hand and twinkled her fingers at them. There were Lucy and Midge—Stuart, too. And next to them Jesse's parents, his friend Craig, forgiven after a heartfelt apology, and his hockey coach. She'd met them all earlier at a lunch generously put on by the Quality Mills Feed company.

It was no wonder Jesse couldn't stop smiling. His parents had promised to support his hockey career after an intense session with his coach and Mr. Devries on the importance of nurturing young talent. In return, Jesse had agreed to go to counselling for a while and make a new start living at home.

"Now I'm going to turn the mike over to the young man who nominated Lancelot for this award. Jesse Sims, please come forward."

Kirsty's mouth opened. She'd wondered who had put forth her pony as a Special Hero. Jesse grinned at her astonishment.

"When I first met Lancelot, I thought he was just an ordinary backyard pony...and not very well behaved. To tell you the truth, I thought he had bad manners because

Kirsty spoiled him too much." He paused while the audience chuckled. "Well, perhaps Lancelot could be better trained, and maybe Kirsty does fuss over him, but the bond between this pony and this girl is so strong he risked his life to save her...and me, too. I've been around a lot of horses and ponies—my grandparents have a ranch and I've spent a lot of time there—but I've never met an animal like Lancelot. He's brave and loyal and smart. And that's why I nominated him for the Special Hero Award."

Photographers and cameramen crouched close, focusing their lenses on Lancelot, but the pony's attention was on Jesse as he spoke. Lancelot ducked his head modestly at the praise and sighed, earning more laughter from the audience.

The announcer took back the microphone and turned to Kirsty. "I understand you bought Lancelot with your own money."

Kirsty nodded.

"And you pay for his upkeep all by yourself."

"I keep him at Hillcroft Farm—that's Lucy and Faye March's place. I do chores to pay for his board."

"Remarkable. Let me pass the mike to Mr. Harry Agnew, president of Quality Mills Feed, The Only Feed You Need, sponsor of the Special Hero Award."

A portly man stepped in front of Lancelot and Kirsty, clearing his throat. "Young lady, let me say it is indeed an honour to meet you. And you…hey!"

The crowd roared as Lancelot gently extracted Mr. Agnew's buttonhole carnation and waved it up and down between his lips.

"Lancelot, no! I'm so sorry. Give that back!" Kirsty tugged the flower away from the pony and handed it back.

"No worries." The company president passed the bedraggled flower to his personal assistant. "Well, Lancelot…or is it Sir Lancelot?"

"Just Lancelot."

"Lancelot, I am very honoured to bestow upon you the Quality Mills Feed Special Hero Award!"

A trumpet flourish blasted over the loudspeakers. Harry Agnew draped over Lancelot a royal-blue blanket with the company's name emblazoned in gold lettering on both sides. He handed Kirsty an enormous silver trophy shaped like a bowl and shook her hand.

"Thank you. Thank you so much," babbled Kirsty. She thrust the trophy into Jesse's hands, then turned to her pony and gave him the signal.

"Well! Well, isn't that something," said Mr. Agnew as Lancelot folded one front leg and bowed deeply before him. "And to you, sir." He bent forward as far as his ample midsection would allow.

The audience cheered wildly while the media rushed in for more photos.

Jesse plucked a long white envelope out of the trophy bowl. "Kirsty, look!"

Inside the envelope was a cheque for a large amount of money from Quality Mills Feed. A very large amount, enough to pay for Lancelot's keep for many years. "I don't understand."

"It's part of the award," explained Jesse.

Kirsty covered her mouth with both hands as the reality sank in. She spun about and flung her arms around Mr. Agnew. "You are the kindest, most generous man...I can't thank you enough."

Mr. Agnew went pink. "You're very welcome. Very, very welcome."

Kirsty released him and stepped back, pink cheeked herself.

"Excuse me! May I have your attention, please!" Laurence Devries held the mike. "I have a special announcement to make."

All heads turned toward him. He set his other hand on Lancelot's shoulder.

"This fine pony's story has a happy ending. But many ponies and horses are living in unfortunate circumstances, through no fault of their own. They are uncared for, unwanted and, in some sad cases, even mistreated. With proper feed and handling and training they could become fine, useful animals, such as Lancelot has become.

"I cannot ignore the plight of these poor creatures. So, at the suggestion of my young friends here, I am establishing the Safe Haven Horse and Pony Rescue."

"A horse rescue. He's starting a horse rescue," Kirsty muttered. "It's like he read my mind...wait, the suggestion of *what* young friends?" She heard Jesse chuckling beside her. "You! You told him!"

Jesse nodded and held his finger to his lips to shush her.

Laurence Devries had more to say. "I envision Safe Havens set up right across this great country of ours. The very first one will be located at Mountainridge Ranch under the care and direction of Midge and Stuart Halliday. As start-up funding I am pledging..."

Kirsty swayed, dizzy at the sum of money Mr. Devries was promising to donate. She propped herself against Lancelot.

There was more.

Harry Agnew reached up and wrestled the microphone from the taller man. "Quality Mills Feed is behind Safe Haven Horse Rescue one hundred percent, and we're going to double Laurence Devries' very generous donation!"

Both men beamed as the audience screeched and stomped its approval. Spooked by the clamour, Lancelot suddenly reared up, pulling the shank through Kirsty's hands. He charged off, galloping free around the huge ring with his head to one side to avoid tripping over the lead shank.

"No, don't chase him. Leave him alone. Please, just stay back!" Kirsty waved everyone away and stepped out into the middle of the ring. She pursed her lips in a shrill whistle.

Down at the other end, Lancelot skidded to a stop. He paused, head high, then whinnied. Spinning around, he raced back across the grass, faster and faster.

"Kirsty, look out! He's going to—"

She held up her hand, and Lancelot slid to a halt in front of her. "Silly old pony." He dropped his head, waggling his ears for her to pull. Briefly, Kirsty pressed her cheek to his neck, one arm wrapped over his neck. Then she gathered up the dangling leather shank.

"Come on, Ponyboy. You're the guest of honour."

Heaving a sigh, Lancelot ambled beside her as they returned to the presentation area.

"That was amazing! Simply amazing!" said Harry Agnew. "One whistle and that pony came right to you! How did you get him to do that?"

"I taught him," said Kirsty. "It wasn't hard—he's very smart. It just took patience and practice."

"You've done a fine job with this pony," said Laurence Devries. "He's a real credit to you as a trainer."

"A trainer? Me?"

"Yes, you, Kirsty. Faye has told me all about you and your pony. How he was bad mannered and barely rideable when you got him. Look at him now. Not only is he well behaved, but he can perform tricks. So did someone else teach this fellow to bow and come to a whistle?"

Kirsty shook her head. "No, that was me."

"Then you're a horse trainer. Oh, you've got a lot more to learn, but one day, Kirsty, you are going to be a very good trainer. I am sure of it."

"Kirsty! Look this way, please," a photographer requested. "Yeah, keep smiling like that!"

As if she could stop. *I am a horse trainer,* Kirsty told herself. *Mr. Devries says so.* She shivered with excitement at the notion. Suddenly, she felt that everything in her life was fitting into place.

"I'm a horse trainer," she said, so softly that only Lancelot heard, his wide ears twitching forward to listen. "I'm going to learn everything I can," she vowed, looking into his deep, dark eyes, "and I'm going to be the very best I can be."

Lancelot gently nuzzled her cheek. And then, unprompted, he slowly dropped down onto one knee, his glossy mane nearly touching the ground as he bowed his neck before her.

About the Author

Julie White started making up horse stories at a young age after her parents told her she couldn't keep a pony in the backyard of their Vancouver home. When she was twelve, her family moved onto a farm near Vernon in the interior of British Columbia, and she got her first horse, a headstrong chestnut named Roger.

Julie lives on a horse farm near Armstrong, B.C. Along with her husband, Robert, a former jockey, she raises thoroughbreds for racing and jumping. She rides every day and competes in jumping classes at horse shows, often against her two grown daughters. Julie is a Pony Club examiner, riding instructor and course designer.

Riding Through Fire is Julie's fourth book, and the third book in the award-winning Hillcroft Farm series. It was inspired by the Cedar Hills fire of 2003 near Armstrong, during which Julie and her husband helped evacuate livestock.